JOHN BINIAS

Theory of Flesh

MACMILLAN

First published 2000 by Macmillan
an imprint of Macmillan Publishers Ltd
25 Eccleston Place, London SW1W 9NF
Basingstoke and Oxford
Associated companies throughout the world
www.macmillan.co.uk

ISBN 0 333 76664 4

1 3 5 7 9 8 6 4 2

A CIP catalogue record for this book is available from
the British Library.

Typeset by SetSystems Ltd, Saffron Walden, Essex
Printed and bound in Great Britain by
Mackays of Chatham plc, Chatham, Kent

To Tanya Crawford

Acknowledgements

For reading, and making comments upon (or remaining mercifully silent about) my manuscript, many thanks to: Tanya Crawford, Paul Clark, James Kean, Martin Membury, Martin Fletcher, Rosi Wightman, Peter Guy, Joyce Binias, Derek Binias, Lorna Crawford, Clare Crawford, Oliver Cheetham, Rupert Girdham, Isabel Tcaciuc, Thomas Bosteels, Colm Long, Anne Scott, Alice Miles, and Suzy Willson. For helping turn the manuscript into a book, particular thanks to Mic Cheetham and Peter Lavery.

(not Quite)

Effulgence of white light. Pain embedded in warmth. Knowledge of joy at no distance.

The psychiatrist, who specializes in cases like mine, says I am to keep a journal, a detailed record of my thoughts, feelings and memories. At present I have only thoughts and feelings. I have decided to do as he suggests, though writing is the last thing I feel like doing at the moment. My skull still throbs from the blow I received.

Because my memories may return without that fragrance of familiarity by which memories distinguish themselves from other mental events, I am for the time being to record everything that occurs to me, even ideas that present themselves as fantasies or daydreams. I rather like the idea that my memories, if improperly labelled, might be mistaken for fantasies. Perhaps I once led a life of excitement? Perhaps I was a glamour-puss? No! One of the few things I am clear about is that I was, and am, one of the least significant forms of human life.

What a melancholy mark is the exclamation! The vertical flees upwards to the freedom of the skies, abandoning its stump and, hidden beneath the line, its nourishing root. Transcendent premonitor of inevitable withering. I shall exclaim no more.

It occurs to me what a strange thing it is to ask of someone that they should record everything that occurs to them. Surely the most complete journal can include only what it occurs to the author to write down?

The medical staff tell me my name is René Quite. The name rings no bells.

I have two doctors. The first supervises the medical checks on my brain. Him I call Doctor Majestic, in honour of his preposterously self-satisfied manner. The second is a psychiatrist. Him I call Doctor Nous, in recognition of the great intuition he imagines himself to possess. Dr Nous comes all the way across town in order to ask me about what he calls my 'mental life'. He finds the human mind endlessly quaint. He is beguiled by it as some folk are beguiled by those silly bottle gardens that can only be tended with special long-stemmed trowels and forks. In both cases the charm would appear to lie in the contrast between the transparency of the container and the awk-wardness of physical access.

Nous was called in when Majestic decided that my amnesia did not satisfy the expectations raised by the nature of my head injury. He is a connoisseur of mental disorders, who specializes in mnemonic peculiarity and takes a collector's delight in rare examples. I believe he spends much of his spare time scouring the region for people who, like myself, have become significantly forget-ful. He is intelligent and not altogether uncultured, but suffers somewhat from literal-mindedness. I suppose as a psychiatrist he is paid to be this way. It certainly wouldn't do if he were to set himself up in competition with his patients for flights of fancy.

Nonetheless, it is irritating. When I told him I enjoyed the idea of my memories being mistaken for fantasies, my irony wholly eluded him. He replied very soberly that fantasies are often painful things, that many of his patients are haunted by cruel imaginings, and that memories, despite what you might expect, can often bring pleasure. For many of us, he insisted, it is only through the judicious exercise of our innate ability to forget suffering and dwell blindly upon pleasures past that life is rendered endurable at all. Indeed, he sometimes wonders whether this is not the case for the whole species of Man. This last thought he expressed with a certain dryness, a fastidiousness of the mouth, as though the words he was uttering were infectious agents which if permitted to linger on his lips a moment too long would envenom his soul. Then he too would succumb to the epidemic of psychic misery he is employed to combat.

But perhaps he fell victim years ago. I suspect this is the case. His manner is strongly marked by the self-conscious vivacity of the chronic convalescent. People are a long time getting over disease of the soul. Bones knit, torn flesh heals, severed nerves regrow, while the eggshell structures of the mind still lie in shards. But what use could a happy psychiatrist ever hope to be to the mentally distressed? Set a thief to catch a thief ...

When Nous asked me if my inability to remember anything before my injury bothers me, I had to admit that it does not. Since I have no idea who I was, surely it would be absurd to regret my passing. The truth is I feel a strange contentment.

The ward is high up, at the top of a tower. One wall is all window, so we get to see a good-sized chunk of sky. What the sky is doing is by far the most important thing. The light occupies me. Pure blue and pure, dense grey define the limits. Can grey be pure? Yes. Between these extremes, infinitely variable patterns of clouds transform the sunlight into infinite modes. Sunlight, as we all know, has no sense and no formal logic, but it does have grammar.

The azure of this morning's dawn was bejewelled with dusty petals of pink ice, which were quickly blanched by the rising sun. Now, bright white puffs of frozen laughter cast playful shadows on great ironic groans of vapour.

The quality of the light which suffuses the ward and steeps our ugly furniture is always a precise figure, the exact solution to an equation of monumental complexity.

At present it is thin, clotted, tart, and a little sour. From the chair beside my bed I gulp down as much as I can. This is my priority.

In the bed opposite is a man of indeterminate age who pleads over and over, at all times of the day and night, to be allowed to die. His name is Mr Barclay. *Why can they not let me be?* Mr Barclay whimpers. *Why do they torment me so? I never asked to be brought here. It is a holy font of shit.* Statements such as these he bellows out reproachfully in his warm and rather lovely Irish brogue. Whether he is referring to the hospital or the planet Earth I do not know.

The nurses are full of contempt for him. One of them makes a stock response to his groaning requests for release, crying out with joyous sarcasm, *How could we let you die when you bring us so much pleasure?* They whisper indignantly that he is not even seriously ill. They have a clear notion of how much woe any particular patient is entitled to express, and apportion their sympathy accordingly. Their system is based upon the belief that people should pull the weight of their health in cheerfulness. Towards this death-intoxicated Irishman they behave as towards a man in a lifeboat who not only refuses to row, but also insists upon beating out a rhythm that confounds the stroke.

Mr Barclay and the nurses have a running battle over analgesia. It follows a fixed pattern. The ritual begins with him impugning the quality of whatever palliative he has been given, declaring peevishly that it has deadened the pain not one jot. Then he demands more. The nurses used to ask a doctor for permission, but the patient has cried wolf too often now, and his complaints go unheard. And so he accuses them of brutality. Perhaps he really is in pain. Something appears to be causing him to suffer.

I sense behind me a fleshy hatred. I turn. Expression of inexorable disdain. Then nothinged, and nothing am.

Some of Mr Barclay's exclamations are extraordinary, almost hilarious. But if his intention is humorous he certainly knows how to keep a straight face. A few moments ago the sun appeared beneath the rain clouds for the first time today. The ward was flooded with an almost glutinous pinkish-bronze light. Everyone in the room who was conscious and physically able inclined their eyes towards the source, except this dour Irishman, who turned his face away as though shying from unwanted pity. After a few moments, he cried out in a voice full of wrath, *Could somebody not turn that fucking sun out once and for all? It gets me in the gut.*

When there is a nurse in the vicinity his expression is always grim. But when he is sure they are all out of the way he will occasionally honour someone with what I take to be his smile. His top lip curls slightly, not upwards at the corners so much as forwards in the middle, as though repelled by the teeth. I have never seen his lower lip join in the festivity. This was the expression he was wearing the first time I clapped eyes on him, soon after I came round. He was watching me intently. When he was sure I was conscious he smiled his crucified smile and called out to me, *How does it feel to be back in the land of the dying?*

He is, I think, genuinely sympathetic towards other

people's pain. Certainly he empathizes. But his concern is combined with a kind of proselytizing enthusiasm for misery which makes one reflect that, while his heart, no doubt, is in approximately the right place, sometimes it is the slightest misalignments that have the most severe consequences.

I asked Nous what he thought the man's problem was. He said he thought he was suffering only from ordinary unhappiness, combined with a severe dose of that extravagance of expression which has long been endemic in the country of his birth. I think Nous's expectation of what constitutes an ordinary level of unhappiness is higher than most.

There is a legal action going on concerning a patient on the ward. If he is to live he needs a heart-bypass operation. But the consultant in the cardiovascular department refuses to give him one, on the grounds that he is too old, the quality of his life too low, and his long-term prospects too poor to make it worth the public's while squandering any more money on his care. Without this operation the man will not last. Perhaps in recognition of this fact he has been given the bed by the window, closest to the light. He himself seems to have no strong feelings on the question of the operation, or if he has he conceals them. But his son, who comes to see him almost every day, is impassioned. He tells his father in detail how the legal struggle is going. The consultant's decision is to be subject to judicial review. The legal attack will turn on the issue of quality of life. The son has evidence that the consultant's assessment of the quality of his father's life was based largely on the fact that he reads only tabloid newspapers. The son takes great pleasure in explaining to anyone who will listen that he himself reads only broadsheets, but that doing so has never brought him so much as a crumb of happiness. Whereas his father is a simple man with simple tastes who will thoroughly enjoy whatever fresh span of life modern surgical techniques can grant him. Looking out of the window, feeding his cat, reading his paper, waving at the neighbours from the bottom of his garden, these pleasures are all his father needs to bring him happiness far in excess of that achieved by busier, richer and better-educated men. Has he not paid a lifetime's worth of tax and National Insurance contributions? Why should he not reap some benefit now? So the son's argument goes. He speaks of his father's happiness with evangelical intensity.

He asked me 'as a philosopher' what I thought of the rights and wrongs of his case. I told him that I did not think there were any rights or wrongs, to his case or any other. I told him that while I respected his conviction that his father is an adornment to public life worth preserving at the nation's expense, I nonetheless sincerely believed that an individual's choice of reading matter was as good a ground as any on which to decide whether or not to spend money on their medical care. Though, I conceded, it is perhaps a little unfair that patients should be admitted to hospital without first being warned of the possible consequences of failing to read the same newspaper as their doctor. I told him that the problem, as I see it, goes far deeper, and that the true source of his pain should be sought not in the isolated fact of this consultant's decision, but rather in our tacit re-evaluation of old age and death as shameful and obscene, together with the creeping conviction (bastard offspring of successful medical technology) that death is not intrinsic to life but alien to it. Would it not be better all round, I continued, if we were to develop a practice more like that of the Inuit people who, when the time came, would gently cast their old folk adrift on an ice floe? Or like the San people of the Kalahari, who placed their defunct elders in a corral of thorn, provisioning them with just enough food and water to keep them comfortable until the lions or hyenas broke through the flimsy barrier and devoured them? In both cases the inevitable parting took place with solemn and grievous regret, after which the young people would continue on their journey, just as their parents before them. In short, I put it to him that the precise date of departure is less important than the quality of the farewell.

This devoted son was so angry he could barely speak. The melancholic Irishman, seeing that I had disturbed the poor man, cried out to him, *Come, come, don't be upset, it is a steaming great shithole of a fucked-up bollocks and he'll probably be glad to get away from the place.* The son left the ward without another word.

Just witnessed an astonishing exchange between the Ward Sister, a stout, firm-fleshed no-nonsense Yorkshirewoman, and aforesaid miserable Irishman. Mr Barclay, for what reason I do not know, chooses to regale the Ward Sister with insistent displays of exaggerated respect, dropping whatever he is doing whenever she is passing in order to proffer glib pleasantries, queasy smiles and feeble gestures of adoration, once even going so far as to genuflect towards her. This dialogue, strange as it was, is not untypical. It went as follows:

MR BARCLAY: (*Confiding tone*) I was happy once, you know, Sister.

SISTER: Were you indeed?

MR BARCLAY: Yes. But it was not all it was cracked up to be. In fact, I thought it was a pile of old bollocks, if you'll pardon my French.

SISTER: (*With a start, as if catching herself in the act of talking to a mollusc*) Why was that, then?

MR BARCLAY: No, it was not at all what I had been led to expect. I think perhaps I have a faulty connection. Up here, you know, Sister. I feel the pleasure all right, but it gives me no joy. Suck my cock and I'll come all over your face like the next man, Sister, but it'd do me no good.

SISTER: It certainly wouldn't, Mr Barclay. I'd see to that myself.

MR BARCLAY: (*Oblivious to the threat*) It's almost as if it were someone else's pleasure and I'm not allowed to touch it. Forbidden. Not the pleasure, you understand, only the enjoyment of it.

SISTER: (*With unconcealed disgust*) You're an unusual man, Mr Barclay.

MR BARCLAY (*With piety*) I hope so, Sister. For humanity's sake, I hope so.

Just shared a waltz with Sue, a sweet young nurse. The television here is left to drone on endlessly in the corner of the room, fulfilling the culturally significant function of preserving us from the burden of our thoughts. The drinking song from *La Traviata* came on while Sue was tidying the bandages on my head. She began swaying her hips to the music. A moment later, without either of us having consciously decided to do so, we were whirling around the ward together. I glanced at Mr Barclay as we swung past him. He looked as though we were dancing on his grave.

Whoever I am, it appears I know how to waltz.

Today, rather slyly, I asked Dr Nous if, in his experience, it was possible, as with other types of disease, to develop immunity to mental illness. He chuckled squirmingly, throwing himself back violently in his chair and clasping his hands against his chest in a deprecatory gesture. What, I wondered out loud, might the psychic equivalent of inoculation be? He himself was such an outstanding example of a *mens sana*. Could it be that psychiatrists, the unwitting milkmaids of the twentieth century, are sitting on some as yet unknown recipe for averting the increasingly common disaster of mental dysfunction? After engaging in a brief and ungainly scrabble to recover his customary cloak of blandness, he finally managed a riposte, quipping perkily that he could see the philosopher in me was aching to get out.

Nous says this kind of thing to annoy me, when I have been badly behaved. I am René Quite, he insists, an academic philosopher at some unimportant university. He forces this identity upon me in an infuriatingly peremptory fashion, as though it were a matter of indubitable fact in which I have no say.

The cause of his absurd belief is as follows. In the library, close to the place where I was found unconscious, were an unattended coat, a wallet, and a briefcase, all belonging to this man René Quite. Understandably enough, the ambulance men presumed that these items were part of the same delivery as the bloodied and beaten semi-corpse they found lying on the floor nearby, and took them along in their ambulance. There being no other information for the hospital authorities to go on, by the time I returned to consciousness some eight or ten hours later it had already been decided beyond a doubt that I was none other than René Quite, lecturer in Philosophy and ally of Aristotle in the ongoing prattling, whingeing and whining contest euphemistically known as Ethical Philosophy. As far as the hospital is concerned I have continued to be this person ever since, despite my protestations.

I can see their point of view, but I cannot agree with it. I retain one memory, and one memory only, from the time before my injury. It is a recollection of pellucid clarity and dire familiarity. I sense someone's presence behind me and spin around just in time to see René Quite, looming above me, large, perhaps larger than life, poised to bring something heavy crashing down on my skull. A brick, a book, a piece of wood, I can't remember what. On his face a look of unquenchable contempt. Then he strikes.

I recognized his face from the photograph on his library card. A mealy-mouthed carping whelp of an academic bellyacher. Not that bad looking. Nothing like me, of course. I have spent some time in front of a mirror. Despite the puffy, blackened skin around the right eye, despite the lumpy scarlet strawberry of a nose, despite the asymmetrically distended right cheekbone, despite the heavy bandaging which conceals my ears, despite the heavy gash on my lower lip and the bee-stung protuberance of my bruised upper lip, despite innumerable small cuts, I recognize myself. Yes, there I am, not Quite, me.

Clearly this man Quite was trying to kill me. Disturbed at the scene and fearing capture, he made his departure in haste, leaving behind him his briefcase, coat and wallet. It is an ill-advised academic who dabbles in practical affairs. The notion of a philosopher king was always an oxymoron for me.

I explained this to Majestic very early on, soon after I surfaced from my little coma. Majestic told me brusquely that this was not what had happened. He called Nous and I repeated my story. Same response, minus the ill manners. Since then we have argued about the issue repeatedly. Nous maintains that the bump on my head is such that it could not possibly have been caused by a blow from the front, that the scene of the accident bore no indication of involvement from any other party, and that one of my university colleagues identified me while I lay unconscious. To which I respond that this so-called colleague may well have been in cahoots with my attacker. In any case, it would hardly be surprising if an unconscious man in a pool of blood should be misidentified. Further, I draw his attention to the fact that the man in the photograph on René Quite's library card resembles me hardly at all. The similarities are gross and extrinsic. At most there is a structural similarity, as between brothers or cousins. Such points of correspondence that do exist serve only to emphasize the points of difference. To this Nous replies that I would be surprised how different a face can seem when the personality that inhabited it has been erased or altered by psychological trauma. He also says that I take too little account of the distorting effect of my injuries.

So far, I admit, Nous gets the best of it. And if there were nothing more to it than this I might be willing to be convinced. But putting aside the memory I have of René Quite assaulting me, and the notable lack of any clear physical resemblance between myself and the man in the picture, I also have the evidence of what I can only describe as my personality. And this personality is most definitely not that of a lecturer in Philosophy. It is not that of a professional intellectual of any kind. Professional intellectuals are self-important people who are afflicted with brutal excesses of intellectual aggression. Their theories are sublimated acts of tyranny. Their desire for truth betrays a deep-seated hatred of life, a gaudy impresario who works by sleight of hand. They would have contradictions reconciled, mixed blessings stratified, right distilled from wrong and the dregs disposed of. They would put an end to the age-old marriage of beauty and terror. They study culture as if it were a parasite on the otherwise healthy vegetable crop of humanity, a nuisance which has only to be thoroughly comprehended in order to be effectively eliminated once and for all.

I mentioned these feelings to Dr Nous. He maintained that it is common for people to have highly critical feelings towards their own careers, and that my strong opinions concerning academia could very well be taken as evidence that, whether I liked it or not, I have had close personal involvement in the scene. In other words he calls a spade a fork with prongs so wide that they join together to form a continuous flat surface highly suited to use as a tool for digging and lifting earth.

While dancing with Nurse Sue, my penis became erect for the first time since I regained consciousness. Sue is shorter than me, nimble and lithe, and managed without contortion to push her belly against my crotch as we were dancing. I know she felt my penis through my pyjamas because when she dropped me back off in my chair she helped me to conceal my enthusiasm with a blanket. She left me with a sweet smile of harmless pleasure. None of the bloodcurdling hunger for flesh that night-shift Jemima betrays every time she comes near a male patient under the age of sixty who is not at that moment suffering a cardiac arrest.

Celebrated difference between Mozart and Wagner.

Swollen warmth, vegetable consciousness, bare flesh stripped, universal hieroglyph, tumescent outcrop of ancient brain, exotic sea creature, phallus, cock, knob. Umbilical conduit of nothing from nowhere to no one.

I only became properly aware of my desire afterwards, when it became necessary to cover it up. Perhaps a consequence of an impaired state of consciousness? All power to it. I desired without desiring satisfaction of that desire. Just didn't get around to it. Still haven't. Unwitting purity of some kind, desire without desire for satisfaction. Even as she moved away from me, her fluent body still singing its exultant song, I remained untroubled. As she left I looked forward with pleasure to the next pleasure, as yet unknown, certain to come soon, sure to be delicious.

No, Nous's argument is captious and inconclusive. Certainly the fact that I have an aversion to academics suggests that I have some experience of them. But what educated person does not? I find in myself an almost equally vehement contempt for politicians, yet nobody is suggesting I am a member of parliament. Nous insists that this latter attitude is so common these days that amongst citizens of Western democracies it passes for normality. Even some of his most confused patients share it, to the point where the occasional individuals who deludedly identify themselves with prominent political personalities often have to be put in seclusion for their own safety. But all that this indicates is a general difference in public levels of familiarity with these two groups of dishonest quibblers, and not, God forbid, that I ever belonged to either of them.

I find the nurses endlessly fascinating. They clean up people's shit and perform the most humiliating tasks, often for aggressively ungrateful patients, yet most of them manage somehow to enjoy their work. It is as if they had formed a pact of sympathy with the human race, a pact which they are determined to keep even if nine hundred and ninety-nine in the thousand have repudiated their side of the deal. But that is wrong. I am making them sound like idealists, which for the most part they very definitely are not. The bargain they make is more Dionysian. They take their pleasures greedily. They take them as they come. Few have qualms about giggling over the torture of an unpleasant patient, just so long as that torture is justified on medical grounds. Most take a robust sensual pleasure in handling the less disgusting patients. Indeed, the one attractive and eligible young male patient on the ward is treated like a pasha in his harem. Anybody who is willing to contribute to the constant struggle to maintain good cheer, with a joke or *bon mot*, is requited with honour and respect. They are profoundly, archaically hierarchical, regarding their favourite doctors with the same petulant adoration that infants lavish upon their flawless parents, and punishing unsatisfactory doctors with correspondingly boundless obstinacy. The depth of their involvement with humanity makes the other people who work on the ward seem wraithlike by comparison.

The melancholy Irishman keeps on repeating that jolly old line from Pascal's *Pensées*:

> *Le silence éternel de ces espaces infinis m'effraie.*

He found it in a dictionary of quotations and has been muttering it as a kind of refrain ever since. If anyone catches his eye he pronounces it to them, either in the original French, or else rendered into English in his own translation.

The always silence of these endless spaces
scares me seven colours of shitless.

But in truth the eternal silence of those infinite spaces is no more terrifying than the silence of the unseen demon who lived under the bed in which I used to sleep in my nanna's house. I knew for sure that if I dallied a moment too long by the bedside he would grab me by the ankle and drag me down to the depths. Yes, in the darkness beneath that childhood bed there dwelled an infinity of evils. It was by their eternal silence that I recognized their maleficence. (Making the bed all the more cosy once I had hopped up into it.)

Stars may beat us hands down for longevity, but they burn themselves out furiously nonetheless. They are no more eternal than we are. And although a human lifespan may seem pathetic compared to that of a galaxy, is not the lifespan of a galaxy pathetic compared to one hour spent in good company, with food on the table, wine in the bottle, and wood on the fire?

How would I know? But I can't help feeling that if a galaxy did have a point of view it would find itself a distressingly transitory affair, lacking in meaning and purpose, and painfully solitary in its being.

Of course the world is eternal and infinite. It has no

outside, no before and no after. I too am eternal, I too am infinite. And I am next to nothing.

The man to my left is dying. His name is Cuthbert. A shapeless great sea cow of a man, he fills his rectilinear hospital bed from edge to edge with blubber. A right-side hemiparesis consequent upon bleeding in the left side of the brain has raised him from the metaphorical class of lardacious mammals to that of gelatinous invertebrates. The image of his jellyfishiness is completed by his pale, translucent skin, through which many colours of vein are visible. This flaccid meniscus hangs so formlessly upon his sagging bulk that he looks as if he had been de-boned in preparation for the sauté pan.

Cuthbert suffers mild panic attacks, which I imagine are caused by his apprehension of his helplessness in the face of Death. He sees that he is running out of life. But he does not allow the gradual elision of his being to interfere with his appetite. The nurses spoon-feed him. His meals are disgusting rituals of open-air mastication. But when they bring the mobile toilet one wishes it were dinner time again, for he evacuates himself with much illustrative grunting and yelping, whether indicative of delight or distress I do not care to know. After a quarter of an hour or so of straining (him to shit, we to occupy our thoughts elsewhere) the ward is filled with his stink. The immortal struggle over, he is scooped up and dolloped back on his bed. The curtains are drawn back and, like something exotic in a fishmonger's window, Cuthbert is returned to the display.

Cuthbert has expressive aphasia, which is to say that what he says makes no sense. But he is able to understand well enough. He smiles a good deal on the left-hand side of his face, particularly in his left eye, and he listens eagerly to the conversations that go on around him. He is especially interested in what Mr Barclay has to say. Cuthbert disapproves of Mr Barclay. This I know because immediately after one of Mr Barclay's pessimistic outbursts Cuthbert's gibberish takes on a distinctly refutative tone. This outraged syllabic *mélange* he directs mainly towards me, Mr Barclay being hidden from Cuthbert's view behind his own vast abdomen. Judging by the look in his eye, I imagine he is summoning oaths of light against Mr Barclay's crepuscular sorrow. Cuthbert likes life.

Dr Nous has been again. Today he explained his thoughts about the therapeutic value of keeping a journal. Literature, he believes, is basically a form of resentment, of feeling old pain afresh. And this is something I need to do more of. Because although my amnesia may be partly organic, some memory loss being a normal consequence of the bludgeoning my cranium received, the pattern of my amnesia is not as it should be. Psychogenetic factors are therefore indicated. In other words, he thinks I've gone mad.

Nous compares psychogenic amnesia to writer's block. The blocked writer is often thought of as someone who is suffering problems with his or her ability to express themselves. In fact the opposite is the case. Literature flourishes under conditions of repression. Far from having difficulties with self-expression, the blocked writer senses the lifting of whatever barrier previously held them back from simple self-revelation, and inspired them to pour out their soul on paper in the first place. Suddenly, anything they need to communicate could be written on the back of a postcard, with space to spare. Literal truth, the death of all art, bears down menacingly upon them. To defend themselves from this cataclysm they stop writing altogether, perhaps even stop speaking, until the threat has passed.

The psychogenic amnesiac, on the other hand, has no career interest in unconscious self-expression. For them, self-revelation is a straightforward question of telling the truth. Unwilling for whatever reason to do this, and unable to turn the writer's trick of detaching the emotional fuse from the explosive object and dealing with each separately, they are forced to repress both together. That is to say, they 'lose' the offending memory. But, as when a liar betrays themselves by dwelling at unnecessary length on the part of their story that happens to be true, a selective editing of memories would only serve to highlight the item that has been left out. And so the amnesiac is forced to adopt desperate tactics, eliminating the pest by burning the entire crop.

So Nous prescribes me a course of expressive activity. Sooner or later, he says, my feelings will show themselves. Maybe at first they will pass themselves off in disguise. Maybe they will impose themselves anonymously upon my perceptions, conspiring to make my present resemble my past, and in that way starting a new life for themselves. For the time being he recommends that I write as much as I can, even trying my hand at fiction if I feel like it. He says I should try to be uninhibited. When I feel ready, I can go back over what I have written and sift it for clues about who I am and how I feel.

But interpretation is a symptom I am keen to avoid. Nous was right to guess that I would never consent to having some libidinous personality critic work off his perverted literary ambitions between the cheeks of my cerebrum. But why did he imagine I would be any more willing to subjugate myself before my own critical faculties? I will keep my journal, but solely for the pleasure of describing the irreducible. I know nothing, and shall remain an avid student of ignorance.

Before I took up my place here my bed was occupied by a teenage boy. He was dying of something rare. The doctors had hoped to save him with a long course of surgical operations. Everyone was agreed that the boy was too young to die. He was too young to have blood on his hands, too young to be accused of the noxious crime of idealism, too young to deserve anything but sympathy.

He was slim and pale with chestnut hair and a whisper of dark fur above his poppy-red lips. Not exactly pretty, though. An inanimate chill hardened his eyes and a curious stillness hung around him, in grim discord with the signs and symptoms of rapid, lopsided adolescent growth.

In societies which suffer from famine, the general practice is to let the children die first. Children are cheaper than adults. They represent a smaller investment of resources and can easily be replaced in times of plenty. Crucially, if the parents are silly enough to let themselves die first, their children will die anyway. Indeed, a gene for dying willingly in childhood could have distinct evolutionary advantages. In the degenerating industrial societies, however, children are the most prized amongst human beings, luxury goods for which no sacrifice is too great. The more useless and helpless they are, the more valuable they are. It is easy to love weak things, is it not? They neither resist us, nor make retreat. That god Jesus was weak, was he not? And the pimps say that he's anyone's. The slapper.

And so children are not allowed to die.

The boy received daily visits from sad, reproachful parents. They could not believe what a disappointment he had proved. Just at the time when he was expected to stand on his own two feet, he had become a child again. They loved him anyway, in a baffled way, astonished that something they themselves had created was able to hurt them so much. The mother was sympathetic, but not too sympathetic because she did not want to make herself cry. If she cried she would be angry. The father was staunch, bearing himself as though he had come to cheer his son on in a game of football. But he did not meet the invalid's eye.

The son himself could not understand what had gone wrong, could not understand why his parents had allowed it to happen. He couldn't decide whether to die, wasn't sure whether dying was not, after all, the grown-up thing to do. In the end he decided in favour and died on his way to the operating theatre, before the anaesthetist could so much as get a needle to him. The next morning his bed was empty. As the sheets were being changed, Mr Barclay shook his big head slowly from side to side, and Cuthbert cried, some say with both eyes. In the afternoon I arrived, out cold.

Developments between the tabloid prophet of heaven on earth and his unhappy broadsheet son. A few minutes ago the son suffered a fit of bilious anger at this stubborn parent of his, who refuses to have anything whatever to do with his own court case. The son accused the father of not standing up for himself, of having always been a docile bastard, of lying down to die like a dog, of being a natural-born victim, of getting no more than what was coming to him, of letting down the side, of not giving a damn about anybody else's feelings, and of reading newspapers that debased his humanity and insulted his intelligence. After his son had left, the father grinned at us. It seems his son's vitriolic attack gave him great pleasure. Perhaps he is proud of his son's ample vehemence. Or perhaps he is simply pleased to find himself capable of having such a powerful effect on his son, even as he struggles for breath and cannot stand without assistance. Yes, perhaps, in his impotence, he finds consolation in tormenting this son of his, who loves him. And perhaps the son wishes to keep his father alive in order that he might console himself in a similar fashion.

I have just been interviewed by Majestic. I informed him that my head is still sore, but the throbbing has stopped. He told me that the swelling has begun to subside and that my vital signs are more than vital enough for me to be up and about again. The five days I have spent here are long enough to enable him to exclude the possibility of complications, and he would be very happy to see me discharged were it not for the continuing problem of my, ahem, memory loss. In view of this he thinks it would be wise for me to remain on the ward for a final consultation with Dr Nous, who will be here tomorrow morning. Since I have no clothes (the ones I was wearing when assaulted having been first steeped in blood and then cut from my body with scissors), I am obliged to accept Majestic's advice.

Dr Majestic appears to regard my case as something of a comedy. He speaks to me with great gravity, as if struggling not to laugh, while at the same time making broad, music-hall gestures to his minions, who smirk obligingly. I am only too happy to provide them with a little fun, they work very hard at what they do. Indeed, I would be perfectly content if Majestic were to laugh openly in my face. I feel well suited to a jester's role, experiencing no resentment in the face of mockery. Indeed, I rather enjoy the attention.

Majestic thinks I am faking it. A good crack on the cranium he regards with respect, while for sub-arachnoid bleeding he has a distinct weakness. But for symptoms in the mind he has nothing but contempt. Nous thinks the mind the most interesting attribute of the human being, Majestic thinks it the least. Indeed, I believe he views it with a degree of suspicion, as if not being purely physical were an embarrassing imperfection. He would probably be happy to be rid of his altogether, if only he didn't need it for professional purposes. I don't suppose he uses it much at weekends.

Whoever I am, it seems I am not very popular. In the five days I have spent here I have received no visitors.

My status has changed. The nurses grow somewhat diffident towards me. Unless I cease resisting their absurd notion that I am a philosophy teacher by the name of René Quite, I suspect I will soon find myself pinned down in one of Dr Nous's specimen cases. I do not find the prospect of spending time on a psychiatric ward at all attractive. I shall have to adopt new tactics.

(I dislike your choice of wallpaper)

I'm out. It wasn't difficult. All they required was that I
should express agreement with all they say concerning who
I am and what has happened to me. I repeated much of it
back to them parrot-fashion. In this way I soon regained
my former popularity. As with books, it would appear that $*$
to be popular you have to tell people what they think they
already know. Yes, of course I'm René Quite, I blathered.
How could I have forgotten that? Thank you so much for
restoring me to myself. For a few days back there, you
know, I felt 'quite' strange. Ha, ha, ha. Not 'quite' myself
at all, ha, ha. Must have been the bump on the head, ha.
And so I wittered on in a knowing-yet-bashful, playfully
pedantic drone, which I assumed especially for the purpose.
I even treated them to a quote from Aristotle:

Call no man happy until he is dead.

I repeated it over and over to anyone who would listen. It was in the battered old dictionary of quotations they have in their sad little collection of broken-backed books. It did the trick well enough.

When Dr Nous arrived to assess me he seemed disappointed. I guessed from this that he had already been given the good news. The lepidopterist in him stifled a cry of vexation as he watched the coveted specimen flitter out of reach of his net. He tried halfheartedly to prove I was faking it. He almost managed it too, having stored away several facts about René Quite of which I remained blissfully ignorant, such as which university I studied at. Oops. I out-trumped him though, asking with innocent curiosity whether the memory must always return in its entirety, like a victorious army, or whether it might not sometimes slink back defeated, in dribs and drabs. Nous had to admit that an incremental return to normality was perfectly possible. I then informed him that I was remembering new things by the hour, that I was looking forward keenly to settling down in my study at 21, Denis Street, where I could be among my books again and continue work on my paper on St Augustine. Quite's home address I read out from the notes in the tray at the end of my bed, which I could just make out from where I was sitting. Nous followed my eyes, and a frank exchange of disingenuous smiles followed.

Even so, he admitted defeat gracefully, asking politely whether I would consent to see him as an outpatient. I do not think I shall. Dissembling is tiring work. Dishonesty,

I hear, is morally wrong. I don't know anything about that. I can make neither head nor tail of what people say about morality. To me it all sounds suspiciously like beating your dog for wagging its tail. But lying to Nous rankled. It isn't that I minded leading him up the garden path. Up the garden path is exactly where psycho-snoopers like Nous belong. But to lie out of necessity is humiliating. In future I shall lie only for fun.

Nurse Sue bought me some clothes, with Quite's money. What do I look like? A loosely-lagged scaffold of bone, the head standing proud, like something erected to commemorate a disaster, the face an arrangement of topographically indistinct features of unclear use-value and scant aesthetic merit. In short, like a man.

Playing along with my mistaken identity was probably not altogether a good idea. I find myself a little lost. In hospital I didn't need an identity. If anything, not having an identity made me an ideal patient. Outside, however, not knowing who you are supposed to be makes it a little difficult to arrange your day.

But my decision was not solely based on my desire to avoid the loony-bin. As I contemplated my position I was struck by the sudden realization that by staying in hospital I may have been placing myself in extreme danger. René Quite tried to kill me once before in a public place. What reason to presume he will not try again? I suppose I could have gone to the police. But what weight could my testimony possibly have, I who cannot even remember my name? Perhaps when I have recovered my memory I will go to them. And then, maybe I will not. For how could I prove that Quite was trying to kill me, and not just to stun or hurt me? The difference lies in the eyes, and they are not justiciable. And what punishment would an apparently respectable middle-class academic receive on a charge of assault? A short suspended sentence at most. And how safe will that leave me? It was me he was trying to destroy, not a policeman, judge or juror. No, I must find my own way of neutralizing this threat.

My life is something I feel very attached to. I find it difficult to express, but there is something inside me like meadow flowers dancing in a light air, or soft leaves tickled by the breath of dawn, or white clouds prancing through wild summer skies. There is a dancing all around me, a dancing and a singing, everywhere I look. The world puts on a most astonishing show. There is so much music.

It occurs to me now and then that I may have done something to deserve René Quite's opprobrium. Perhaps I caused him some injury, for which his action was justifiable retaliation. But in truth I cannot believe I would do anything to provoke such animosity. I have such a placid temperament. I am very willing to please, and easily pleased by people in their turn, just so long as they are not cruel. As for evidence of cruelty in myself, I find little. When a patient on the ward suffered pain I felt unhappy, and to a certain degree I suffered with them. And when, with gleeful malevolence, a nurse crushed a wasp against the window, I found her very ugly. The hum of the wasp's wings, the dynamism of its flight, the rich golden livery of its filamented body, all this was beautiful. I allowed it to alight on my arm for a moment. They do not sting if you do not threaten them.

No, I cannot believe I did anything to deserve what René Quite did to me. And so I intend to revenge myself. I will not torture him, for I am not cruel. But I will destroy him.

I will destroy him, for he lacks beauty.

Nurse Sue gave me her phone number, in case I need her help. She seemed sorry when nobody came to pick me up from the hospital. I think she saw that I was having the doctors on about recovering my memory. I am not sure whether her interest in me is motivated by sympathy, friendship or sex. Perhaps it is a mixture of the three. Or perhaps she is attracted to my lack of identity. Perhaps, as when one visits an unknown country, there is a little more room for the subliminal play of fantasy.

Having no identity is fun for me, too. Though, walking from the hospital to the café in which I am now seated, I did, every now and then, get into a little difficulty. A simple matter of coming to a stand-still every dozen or so paces, not daring to move for dread of what the next step might bring, as though any sudden movement, any movement at all, might cause reality to split open and swallow me up. It is as if I were playing *What time is it, Mr Wolf?* with an irate god. Then the spasm passes and I move on much as before. It surprises me how little attention people pay to this involuntary eccentricity.

Am I mad? But 'mad' is someone else's word, fear of madness fear of what others might say and do to me. So I'll leave it to them to decide.

I have with me René Quite's briefcase and wallet. I have been practising his signature, so that I can use his credit cards, and write cheques on his account. It only took a few minutes to get it right. I think the waitress saw what I was doing though, so I had better pay in cash.

The briefcase contains a lot of notes about philosophy, some of which are in ancient Greek, which I cannot read. René Quite, it seems, is much occupied by the distinction between ethical and aesthetic judgements. He writes: *I dislike your choice of wallpaper. I think it is a bad choice, and in the context of the room in question I believe the choice was objectively wrong. But it would be wrong of me to punish you for it, and wrong of me to use force to compel you to replace it with a more appropriate selection.* It would appear from his jottings that aesthetic judgements are judgements of the suitability of home furnishings, while ethical judgements are concerned with the appropriateness of physical violence. The question of whether violence is apt fascinates him. One gets the distinct impression that he is searching for opportunities to indulge himself.

According to Professor Quite, the most important task our culture faces is re-establishing the rational supremacy of ethics. Experimental science, it seems, undermined our established systems of ethical reasoning early in the modern period by championing a paradigm for rationality which appeared to invalidate all other forms of reasoning. In principle, thinks Quite, all rational people should be able to come to agreement about what is right and what is wrong. Bringing this state of affairs about is the true purpose of education. Only when this has happened can a new politics arise, a politics based not on irrational manip-ulation but on reason. Whereas contemporary so-called democratic so-called politics is the brutal assertion of the material interests of the bourgeoisie, which they accomplish by means of systematic duplicity, the propagation of mass imbecility, an instrumental nurturing of certain vices, together with a light sprinkling of overt acts of violence.

Everywhere he looks Quite sees the irrational domination of one person by another. The spectacle of our ethically debased society fills him with disgust. He believes we are off our collective head, and his goal in life is to restore us to reason. Personally, I suspect he has things arsy-versy. I suspect it is he who is raving, he who must be restored to reason. Haunted by visions of unnecessary suffering, vile tyranny, base deception and squandered potential, he contrasts the woeful state of things as they are with a world which he himself admits has only ever existed imperfectly, adumbrated by transient flourishings, themselves fertilized by the mire that preceded and surrounded them. He postulates a fantasy planet, populated with fantasy people, who will resolve conflict rationally, realize their potential every time, use violence and deception only as a last resort, and be utterly bemused by the very notion of tragedy.

Quite seeks the algorithm for this perfect world, the philosophers' stone that will transform our leaden natures into gold. And his method is to publish short papers in obscure academic journals. No wonder he is unhappy.

At the end of a series of notes concerning what he calls the absolute nature of ethical judgements, he declares triumphantly, *No! When faced with the Holocaust, or indeed any act of human cruelty, only a moral judgement will do.* Sadly for his argument, he does not say what it will do. He dare not say what he thinks because it is too absurd. Underlying his work is the childish belief that moral judgements are a kind of magical incantation, abracadabras which, intoned in the correct manner, will make all the difference between heaven and hell.

Better to die in the right than live in the wrong, he says, without making it clear whether he is talking of interior decoration or ethics.

I know now that when Quite made the above declaration he must have been talking of morality, because where interior design is concerned he very much lives in the wrong. I am in his house now, and I can say with apodeictic certainty that his choice of furnishings is obscenely drab.

I am sitting at Quite's desk, in Quite's study, upstairs in the terrifyingly characterless Thirties semi which I imagine he must, for want of a better word, call home. It forms part of a gridlock of identical, bay-fronted houses that clogs the whole area. The street curves, but without conviction, as if the people who built it had simply wandered off-course through lack of interest in the job. As one walks past the houses, the same bland reality is revealed over and over, as in some obscure, frigid nightmare. If anything, Quite's semi stands out from the others as bearing even fewer than average signs of individual taste. It is almost impossibly anonymous. One imagines the owner's primary goal in life must be to avoid standing out from the crowd. Strange ambition in a man to whom the crowd has proved such a big disappointment. Perhaps he is afraid they will sense his disapproval and take their revenge.

I do not think the neighbours saw me come in. I was wearing Quite's raincoat and carrying his briefcase. At a distance I would have been indistinguishable from the man himself. But if a neighbour had approached me while I was walking up the drive then there might have been trouble.

Being within Quite's domestic penetralia gives me a curious feeling of satisfaction. I have been rummaging through his papers to see if there are any references to me, or to anyone who seems familiar to me. But would I even know if I came across a photo of myself? Would I recognize a reference to my name? If I found a letter from myself, in my own handwriting, would I be any the wiser? It probably doesn't matter, because there is almost nothing here of a personal nature. Everything is academic, everything *as if*. Notes, papers, books, correspondence, even the decor is theoretical. A poor simulacrum of a late twentieth-century middle-class home, fabricated for a museum of social history.

The walls of his study are adorned with a series of grim, faded etchings depicting the faces of the great philosophers. Pride of place is taken by a man called Socrates, whose fat cheeks, squat forehead, flat face, desirous mouth and denying eyes are orchestrated in their ugliness by the infinitely questioning look of a rejected infant.

Except for some decaying dairy products in the fridge there is no evidence of recent habitation. Unopened correspondence congests the hallway. I can't decide whether to remain here or not. Waiting for Quite to return, which sooner or later he must, seems the most foolproof way of finding out what I need to know. And once I know what I need to know, I'll know what to do.

I expect I shall simply resume my previous life. But I wonder why no one has come looking for me from there? From my previous life, I mean. Perhaps I have few friends. Perhaps I have none. Perhaps I have many, but they don't know where I am. I wonder if I am on a missing persons list? How should I find out? Is it possible to apply to a missing persons bureau, in search of oneself?

But what if Quite has gone into hiding? It could be months before he shows his face. I find this place oppressive. It is a lifeless place. And I find I am yearning for Nurse Sue. That, of course, will lead me nowhere. And I would dearly like to be led somewhere, I who have the leading role in this drama of anonymity, without so much as a genre convention to help me.

Perhaps it is time to take the plunge. But what is it to be? A revenge tragedy? A detective story starring an implausibly soft-boiled hero? A tale of existential serenity in the face of a charmingly meaningless existence? Demonstrate, yet again, the futility of prideful vengeance? Prove, yet again, the efficacy of instrumental reason? Or evoke, yet again, the absurdity of a life that eschews the former in favour of the latter? The choice is mine.

Glory be.

(the best castles are constructed along very different principles)

On the slow train to Scarby-at-Sea, changing here, there and everywhere, trundling dully on through the parched ochres and charred greens of late summer.

I did spend the night in René Quite's house. For want of anywhere better to go, and on the off-chance that the great man himself might put in an appearance, I slept in an upstairs room, seated on the floor, with my back against the wardrobe and a clawhammer at the ready by my side. Before going to sleep I arranged a heap of household goods in such a way that they would topple over and crash to the floor the moment the front door was opened, thus alerting me of Quite's presence. I fell asleep fantasizing of cracking his skull with the hammer. I would have preferred a blunter instrument, something less likely to cause death upon the first impact, mainly because I wanted to ask him a few questions before he went. But I could find no more suitable tool in the house. So I planned to disable him with a blow to the scapula, followed by a shattering blow to the knee, or the foot, whichever presented itself as the easier target. The prospect of interrogating the man while he was blinded with pain did not greatly appeal, but sometimes you have to make the best of a bad job.

Nobody came.

The next morning, after having prepared for myself a small cooked breakfast from items I found in the freezer, I continued my search of the house. In a drawer near the telephone I discovered Quite's appointment diary. My first big stroke of luck. And in the diary I discovered a hotel booking. A fortnight at the Grand Hotel, Scarby-at-Sea, starting in two days' time.

Quite is sure to know that I have left the hospital. He will guess that I am hunting him. What better place to track him down than in a holiday resort, amongst crowds of strangers? I doubt he will be on the lookout for me there. Whereas if I attempt to find him at the university, where he knows his way around and I do not, I would draw attention to myself immediately. My face is still rather swollen and bruised. In fact I don't look at all normal. My skull is misshapen. Everything seems to have gone a little pointy.

I had two days to kill. I killed them with Nurse Sue.

When I went round to her flat I was worried that she would be keen to discuss with me exactly who I was. I was very relieved when she showed only polite interest in the question. Her attitude to my loss of identity was not at all censorious. She leads an immediate life, sustained not by the demands of so-called reality but rather those of subjectivity – hers and other people's. She has dreamy turquoise eyes, the irises limned in black. They underline the things she likes. When I spoke to her of my predicament, she received any hypothesis I offered concerning my identity with a minimum of fuss. She approved some ideas and rejected others with as little anxiety as if we had been in a costumier's shop, and I were trying on the various outfits. I think it is probably true to say she was more interested in how I smelt than who, if anyone, I was. How I smelt and how I tasted told her all she needed to know. Of course, she was also interested in how I behaved. But since I liked the way she smelt and tasted, the little kindnesses flowed without effort.

While Sue was at work I spent more time sifting Q's transcendental ramblings for signs of life. I find perusing the contents of my enemy's mind a curiously entertaining diversion. I now feel competent to draw some general conclusions about the man. I am sad to say he has a distinctly inferior intellect. I feel rather ashamed to have been bopped by such a man. He is a brute secular salvationist.

In one of his notebooks he defines the goal of his philosophical enquiry as answering the question *How, objectively speaking, should a human being act for the best?* But why on earth should anyone be interested in giving an *objective* answer to this question? What sort of life a person should live is surely every bit as personal a question as what sort of painting a painter should paint. An objective answer only exists where there is a pre-existing market for a particular type of product. In our society there exists no such market, either in paintings or in humans. Long ago or far away, perhaps, but not here and not now. René Quite wants society to behave as though it had a purpose. But society is a rich, selfish, aimless old fool whose only joy in life is in doing down the neighbours. What need does such a society have of René Quite's rational virtues?

The truth is that Quite lives in fear of criticism. His passion for objectivity is the mirror image of his terror of being in the wrong. He brandishes his morality at the world, demanding that it should approve of him. He is about as rational as a gardener who tries to fell a tree with a set of spanners.

Scarby-at-Sea is one of those Victorian seaside resorts whose romantic charm increases as its public popularity wanes. It is compounded of cracked plaster, blistered paint, creeping rust, spongy wood, and the tiny tragedy of an ice-cream fallen on hot tarmac. This year, I am told, is a bad one. I mean a particularly bad one. The long beaches, large pleasure gardens and wide esplanades have the lugubrious, contented, yet faintly hysterical calm that I imagine might afflict a reluctant prostitute who suffers a drastic fall in trade, and whose returning self-respect is offset perfectly by their growing fear of poverty.

I found the Grand without difficulty. It is located on the top of the cliff that runs behind the quieter of Scarby's two bays. In elevation it lies midway between the scrubbed beach and the high plateau on which the crumbling castle totters. The hotel itself is both larger and more decayed than its brethren. Twelve windows wide by ten windows tall, it boasts well over a hundred bedrooms, most of which are empty from one year's end to the next. The exfoliating baby-blue stucco exterior and the sun-soured vermilion curtains speak in stage whispers of impending closure.

Having located the hotel I realized I had no idea what to do next. I mean no idea at all. For a while I stood looking at the entrance, waiting for something to happen. Nothing did. I retraced my steps down the grassy cliff and went out onto the beach, hoping to find inspiration in the sea.

A diaphanous morning haze clung to the sky like the dusty bloom on some great blue fruit. The sea was a smudgy, undistinguished grey, the waves languid and sapped of energy, their mechanical whisking and slithering vaguely suggestive of migraine. The tide was out and acres of wet, palpy sand lay denuded.

It was ten in the morning when I arrived. By ten-fifteen the sun had gathered its strength and the mist was spirited away. Silken rays of light touched life into the scene. Spangles of water were made and marred in their trillions as the waves beat out shuffling, swerving rhythms on the shore. Scholarly gulls described their favourite arcs against invisible axes in the sky, crying out deafly to one another of their deep reservations and their dubious joys.

Strolling by the water's edge, I became aware that bit-by-bit these pristine sands were being colonized. Each party was in the process of setting out their little camp, a more or less compact dwelling place precisely defined against the expressionless expanse by carefully placed rugs, towels, windbreaks, chairs, sunshades, hampers, and nets. While the camp is being established, the infant members of the party scour the surrounding area for significant aberrations in the vast blank of the seashore. Protruding rocks, unusual shells, ancient driftwood, inexplicable ripples and creases, a freshwater rivulet that cuts into the sand and creates bluffs and creeks, islands and deltas of epoch-defying brevity, all these features help characterize the spirit of the emerging nation. Only when the topography has been thoroughly reconnoitred, and the camp erected and provisioned, can work on the sandcastle begin.

The game of sandcastles has a twofold aim. That is to say, the game falls into two distinct stages. During the first stage the players devote themselves, body and soul, to erecting an edifice of which they can be properly proud, an ideal fortress or sanctuary in which one might rest safe from elements both natural and human. The construction work completed to the most exacting standards, the second part of the game begins. In an ecstasy of laughing grief, swelling humility, and shrinking pride, the players look on as the dwelling of their hopes is first licked, then nibbled, then gulped down whole by the hungry, disinterested tide.

A word on technique. Contrary to what some people think, the best sandcastles are not those wide, low constructions with deep moats and massively thick walls, designed solely with the purpose of resisting for as long as possible the onslaught of the ocean. This type of castle is essentially tragicomic. It is built mainly by teams of infants headed by hysterical young adult males with loose teeth and lots of nervous energy. These men lack sensitivity to the poetry of the game they imagine themselves to be playing, and take the notion of constructing a defence against the encroachment of the sea quite literally. Starting as early as possible, and as close to the high-tide line as they can, their fundamental mistake is to strive with all their might towards a goal which they already know to be impossible. If they reflected they might even realize that such a goal is not even desirable. One imagines this type of player, given the resources, cheerfully employing mechanical diggers, concrete pillars and corrugated steel barriers in their desperation to prove that they can prevail.

The infants themselves, of course, are inevitably disappointed. Because, while it is impossible not to be impressed by such a generous outpouring of energy, warped hopes lead only to despair, and children see this. Yes, the offspring of such Canutes may stand amidst the inexorable waves with dry tootsies for a minute or so longer than other children on the beach. But so what? They know far better than their imbecilic fathers that they could have had dry tootsies anyway, had they sincerely wanted them, simply by moving up the beach ahead of the tide. Such hubris ends in shame, as the whole garrison is forced to decamp through deep water, possibly even getting their shorts wet in the process.

The best castles are constructed along very different principles. The trick lies in achieving as delicate a balance as possible between aspiration and its inevitable defeat. To allow hours to pass between creation and decay would be to humiliate ambition with opportunity. But to set out upon a project so demanding it must inevitably be washed away before completion causes only grief. As with any good narrative, failure must chase hard upon the heels of success if tedium and absurdity are to be defeated. Children know this and, left unfettered by the dim-witted ministerings of adults, will naturally tend to the creation of lofty, ornate structures bursting with desirable features such as drawbridges, crenellated turrets, boiling-oil ducts and sunny courtyards. They will build until the last minute, timing things so that the decorative work comes to completion just as the brine comes coursing into the moat. Then they watch avidly as another perfect world is washed away by the pitiless sea.

I observed one builder, particularly expert and committed to his art, who was struggling to discover coordinates on the land by which he could fix the position of his castle. He wanted to be able to find the exact spot the next day, so that he could check that the sea really had brought his enchanted citadel to nought, restoring the beach to its customary state of desolation. Everything suggested it would do so, nothing suggested otherwise, but nonetheless he craved proof. Had proof been forthcoming, he would no doubt have craved proof of that proof. Proof that his coordinates had not shifted, proof that he had walked onto the same beach, proof that he had woken into the same world, proof that he had woken up the same boy. So much can change from one day to the next. Nothing is fixed. Children know this.

On the beach the human gaze reaches to the horizon, and one can find oneself in curiously intimate contact with people hundreds of yards away. It is a zone of utmost exposure. The only hiding place is beneath the waves. A child can wander anywhere, safe in the knowledge that their world will continue to be supported by their mother's fond eyes. And yet, at the end of each day, the beach is buried beneath the water, the light is submerged, and human eyes have no more power than pebbles.

Thinking of children reminds me of a remark of René Quite's in which he says that nobody who is truly moral, who refuses on principle to cause unnecessary human suffering, could ever approve of having children. For what more reliable method of preventing human suffering is there than contraception? What better anaesthetic could there be than not being conceived? He is right. A life without suffering is not on the menu. But so what? What's so bad about suffering? His remark only goes to show what a useless interpretation of the notion of goodness this man has saddled himself with.

Before I forget, a word or two about my knife. I bought it under the counter from a shop that specializes in selling all things disreputable, distasteful and mildly illegal. The shopkeeper, a short, generously moustached man in his early forties, had about him a tragic look of lost liberty, as though eternally imprisoned in his own miserable soul, only able to view the world through the iron bars of his unappealing personality. The root of his tragedy, or the fullest expression of it, appears to be his powerful and obsessive affinity with all things banned, censored or otherwise disapproved of.

When I told him of my need for a weapon of self-defence he initially offered me a powerful crossbow, a tool which, he gleefully informed me, was capable of sending a steel-tipped bolt through a half-inch plank of oak. As he explained this, he gave me an irresponsible leer that was clearly intended to communicate to me just how little he cared for the standards of respectable society. I told him that he was overestimating the magnitude of the danger I was facing. He replied that he very much doubted that he was. I was struck by the notion that one day he or one of his paranoid customers might just fire one of those pencil-thick bolts at me, and was very tempted to shoot him with the damned thing there and then, through the belly for preference, ridding the world of a potential evil and at the same time wiping the look of abject smugness off his face. Needless to say, this idea was quickly chased away by premonitions of blood, of shrieks, of screeching sirens, and of many dull years spent in prison.

Next he showed me a sharp metal star for throwing at people, a sort of death frisbee. When I rejected that he brought out an underwater harpoon. These items appeared to have great resonance for him, hieratic symbols of the personal liberation about which he dreams. Next, he showed me a catapult that fired heavy steel balls, then an extendable steel spring with a weight on the end. Then he tried to sell me several types of rice-flail. Eventually, as I was about to leave, he brought out his selection of knives.

The one I chose is very beautiful. It has a slim steel blade some five inches long that is shaped like a blade of grass and is the colour and texture of white silk. The blade is sheathed between two troughs of metal which fold back to form a handle. It was, the man told me with deviant joy, primarily intended for stabbing with. If I was interested in slashing I should consider something with a thicker blade. Stabbing sounded fine to me; I wouldn't know how to slash, I am an all-or-nothing kind of man.

Resisting the temptation to put the knife to the test then and there, something which the shopkeeper, with his intolerable gloating, seemed almost to be daring me to do, I paid the sum he demanded, slipped the knife into my pocket, and left.

(the philosopher has fallen silent)

It turns out my story is to be a romance. Yes, I am in love. Whoever I am, I am in love.

I will try to bring myself up to date. I stayed on the beach until late afternoon. When the tide had once again taken possession of the shore and the families retreated to the esplanade, I made my way to a café, where I had fish and chips followed by vanilla ice cream. Then I decided to ring the hotel and find out if Quite had arrived yet. I made the call, asking innocently if it was possible to speak to one of their guests, a Mr René Quite. The receptionist hesitated, then informed me that Mr Quite had not yet checked in, but that he was expected that evening and if I rang back later I would probably be able to speak to him. I declined to leave a message.

I wandered up and down the shore for a while, asking myself over and over what was the most sensible thing to do. Once again my mind was a blank. I stopped walking and stared at the sky. A few moments later I understood. By trying to act sensibly I was taking the wrong approach. For someone with no known past, with no plans for the future, with no personal identity beyond some disparate feelings of like and dislike towards unrelated objects, someone whose sense of reality is attenuated to the point of ecstasy, sensible behaviour was probably not possible. It probably wasn't even sensible.

The principle of impulsive action thus enthroned in my mind, I walked boldly back along the foreshore and up the grassy cliff to the Grand Hotel. Still panting a little from the sharp climb, I passed through the rotating mahogany and glass doors and into the lobby, where I found a large, friendly-looking man waiting to greet me. He was wearing a dress shirt and black dickey-bow, under a moth-gobbled cardigan the colour of donkeys. His legs were covered to just below the knees by green tweed breeches. Long socks hung loose at his ankles, leaving his calves bare.

This big dapper character was the proprietor of the hotel. His name was Effie Rance. On first apprehending Mr Rance I was struck by the thought that he was a man of wisdom. Rotund and gently perspiring, his folds of fat and pendulous jowls were rendered acceptable, attractive even, by an animating quickness of humour and a great warmth of demeanour. He gave the impression of having recently eaten a rich meal with heavy sauces, which he was presently occupied in digesting. So powerful was his air of generosity one could almost imagine that he was digesting someone else's meal too, perhaps as a favour to a dyspeptic guest.

He could conceivably have been a policeman in a former incarnation, a big bouncing bobby on the beat. But if so, like a bishop who renounces God at his retirement luncheon (the bishop's that is), he had well and truly given up the faith. For he resembled a policeman not at all. Nor did he resemble an ex-policeman, as that term is generally used. For he bore no trace of peevishness, showed nothing but approbation for human weakness, betrayed no desire to be right, no desire to be wrong, no interest in the letter of the law and even less in its spirit, and evidently felt no need to justify either his actions or his existence. In fact he showed only an overarching concern for reconciliation, good humour, good digestion and peaceful sleep. If Nature still lived, this man would be at one with her. If God had ever existed, no doubt there would have been differences of opinion, but things being what they were, he had a clear run.

So what was there of the policeman about him? Absolutely nothing whatsoever. He was, in short, neither a serving policeman nor an ex-policeman but a not-policeman, the perfect negation of a policeman, and it was precisely this complete lack of policemanliness, this utter dissimilarity to a boy in blue, which was so reminiscent of one. If a policeman, erect in his helmet, occupies a certain space, then this man, this proprietor, occupies the rest of space, encompassing and embracing all. All, that is, save a small but very significant hollow deep inside him, the exact size and shape of a uniformed copper,

truncheon poised in readiness to wean some breezy innocent from their pleasure with blows. So the two concepts,
policeman and proprietor, defined each other in my
imagination.

For want of a better alias I checked into the hotel
under the name René Quite. After giving me the key to
my room the proprietor told me that Scarby-at-Sea was a
resort of pleasure and I should feel free to enjoy myself as
I thought fit. As he uttered this strange formula of
welcome I noticed myself reaching in the pocket of my
jacket for my knife.

Curious feeling of expectation.

With what I suspect was rather a guilty smile I left the
proprietor at reception and went upstairs to my room. It
has a sea view. I am in it now, crouched over an undersized
writing table, glaring at the ocean. It has in it ... but why
would I want to describe the room I am sitting in? It has
in it two things, furniture and space. The other contender
for itemhood, which is to say myself, I take to be a kind
of hybrid of the first two, and of no ontological
significance.

I did not unpack my bag on arrival, which anyway
only contained the few items of clothing I had bought
earlier in the day, together with various bits and pieces of
written material taken from Quite's briefcase and study.
Instead I locked the door, moved an armchair over to the
window, opened my knife, lay it upon the arm of the
chair, took out this journal, and proceeded to read over
everything I had written so far.

I found that my journal is littered with generalizations,
observations and arguments of an impersonal kind. In fact,

I find myself unpleasantly opinionated. But that is beside the point. Apart from my recollection of being walloped on the bonce by René Quite I found only one example of a distinctively personal memory. Something about the bed I slept in at my grandmother's house. And yet, when I wrote that, I did not even know I had a grandmother. Not that I could not have guessed as much if the question had been raised. But that white-sheeted bed beneath which devils lurked? All recollection of it has gone. But do we ever remember anything more than once? Is the second time around not always a memory of a memory? And what linked the memory to the bed? It could have been festering in my mind for years, undergoing some organic process of transformation. Might it not have started life as a joke about a prelate who forgot to return his grandmother's bicycle?

And who knows whether it was even a memory when I first wrote it down? I could have been confabulating to illustrate the point I was making. It could have been something I read in a book. Books are so much more convincing than reality, which in my experience has a hollow ring to it, lacks polish and has no clear storyline. No, there is nothing, absolutely nothing that connects me with my past.

By the time I had finished playing the critic it was early evening. Not yet ready to eat, I remained slumped in my seat, watching the sun sputter and die, the sky subside, and the darkness rise. It wasn't really dark, though. It was more a meagre soup of stringy, leftover bits of light. I switched on a lamp and picked up a folder full of brochures advising of the entertainments Scarby offers its internees. These seemed a measly, intelligence-defying array of trumped-up opportunities for cynical tradespeople to relieve honest tourists of their disposable income, including imprisoned dolphins, any number of mechanical devices for inducing vomiting in small children, pathetically undersized steam trains, potteries, fudge manufactories, potteries, reptile collections, and potteries, to name but six, one of them three times.

I was reflecting on the baleful inanity of such occupations when something very unusual happened. Unusual then, not so unusual now. What had a moment before seemed a panoply of opportunities for feckless time-wasting was imperceptibly transformed, as if by some obscure process of inversion, into a rich and subtle array of harmless, charming, inconsequential but nonetheless fascinating diversions.

Then I became aware that there was someone in the room with me, standing behind my chair. This person, whose breath I could now feel on my neck, was interfering with my world. I was about to reach for my knife when they spoke to me.

'I say we start off at the pleasure gardens.'

It was a woman's voice. Dark and dusty like a cello, smooth like a clarinet and clear like a tabla, it inflamed me with the desire to be whispered to. I turned.

To say of someone like Eugenia that she is beautiful is to concede too much in the way of comparability. Yes, with Eugenia generic terms can only send the imagination in the wrong direction, she is so very particular. Her fluid hair catches the light and twists it into purls. Her skin is new and alive as velveteen fungus (if fungus can be

allowed for a moment to be beautiful). Her face is sensitive to all that she is sensitive to. New-born feelings
seem always to be frolicking there. She looks perfectly
herself, the picture of herself, and she sounds herself too,
sounds the song of herself. In Eugenia, for the first time
in the history of metaphysics, phenomena and noumena
coincide. She expresses herself fully, even when standing
calmly in silence. She sees with her eyes closed and she
thinks with her fingers. She has a deliquescent soul. She
views the world in at least three dozen discrete shades of
emotion, so that her perception appears richer and more
interesting than the world she perceives. What I am
saying, I suppose, is that her world is more interesting
than mine. And so, unless I am allowed to be a part of
her world, to share her perception of the world, I feel all
sucked off.

Eugenia is keeper of the synaesthetic keys, my sensual
and spiritual gaoler. But my experience of her absence and
presence do not correspond with her physical absence and
physical presence. I suppose this is to say, I am haunted
by her. When she is absent the world grows indistinct,
myopia overwhelms me, and the bright goo of my visual
field is as far as perception will take me. When she is
present, spirits leap from the trees, all is animated and
gods abound. Yes, gods abound. But do not imagine she
worships them. No, it is they who worship her. Day and
Night, Sun, Moon, Stars, Sky, Sea and Earth, Love,
Horror and Death, all worship her and do her bidding.

I am running ahead of myself, like a schoolboy eager
for the honours. And perhaps I am exaggerating a little,
weakening my case by overstating it. But the world with

Eugenia seems more real than the world without, in the sense in which a TV image with good reception and bright, lifelike colours captures more reality than one with poor reception and indistinct images. And then it seems less real too, in the sense that the gist of the narrative seems not to conform to expectations. Enchantments and every imaginable sort of uncanniness abound. It is a new form of life, not yet matured into a genre, and I live in fear of returning to the pasty realism that preceded it.

To resume. I spun around to see Eugenia smiling at me, amused by my startled face. She moved over to the window. While her back was turned I slipped my knife down the side of the chair. She turned to face me, leaning her hands against the sill. I felt the need to speak but could not, for I was choked, and somewhat melted, and tormented by curious, ill-formed impulses, as though I were silently stuttering, stuttering with my whole body. I have come to know this feeling well. Eugenia draws emotions from me as the sun coaxes primroses from the muck. I try to prevent them, but one way or another they make an appearance, pushing through my clods and stony rubble, out into the warmth. Seeing that my lips were pressed together and that I had no intention of speaking, Eugenia filled the silence herself.

'How are you?' she asked.

I couldn't utter a word.

'So, the philosopher has fallen silent. My goodness. All right, I'll talk. I'm well. I've been busy. I'm selling a lot. I've bought myself a new car...'

'Who are you?' I blurted out. Or did I purr? Did I in fact purr, with pleasure and amazement? I suspect I did. I would have preferred to have blurted, it would have been less revealing. Even at that early stage I was afraid to acknowledge that I had fallen under her spell. And equally unable to refrain from doing so.

'I'm your wife, dear. Your wife, Eugenia. Your wife of eleven years, recently thankfully estranged.' Her voice contained a hint of bitterness.

'What have you been selling a lot of?' I asked.

'Paintings, of course. What is wrong with you? Why are you grinning like that?'

'Because you're so beautiful.'

'René...'

'René?'

'What is wrong with you?'

'You called me René?'

'I'm finding your behaviour rather obscure,' she said somewhat severely. As she spoke she looked towards the door. I felt the need to make some sort of explanation. It was difficult to know where to start.

'I don't know what to say,' I said.

'You know, I've never heard you utter those words before. Not in that order, anyway. Either you've changed, or I've got the wrong room.' Her wide roses-are-red lips released a peal of creamy giggles back into the wild, and her bright eyes conjured up a sweeping panorama of absurdity. I found myself hoping we might live there together in motley, daftly ever after. Being ridiculed by such a woman seemed a rare honour. Indeed, the idea of being murdered by her was not without its attractions, if it pleased her to do so. I decided to take the plunge.

'I had a bang on the head and don't know who I am

any more. I thought it was René Quite who hit me. I thought he was trying to kill me.'

She came over to me and put her hand gently on my head. At first I thought that she was giving me a kind of benediction. But she was looking for the bump. She found the spot without difficulty; a clump of hair was still missing. When she touched it I flinched. She hesitated, looked at me from a distance, then bent over and kissed it better. It hurt when her lips touched it, but it felt better all the same. Only, I wanted her to do it again, and this wanting was rather sore. She didn't oblige. In fact she seemed already to regret this show of tenderness and quickly returned to her place by the window. Her scent lingered on. I say scent, but it was more an olfactory emotion than an odour, as in spring when the sun's glance first warms the oily buds.

'When did it happen?'

'About two weeks ago.'

I explained to her that I remembered seeing a man about to hit me, then nothing until waking up in hospital. I told her how the doctors had insisted that I was a philosopher, a notorious lover of truth by the name of René Quite, and that I didn't believe them. I explained that I had read René Quite's books and disagreed with almost everything he thinks.

This made her smile. 'Well, that sounds like you. You always were contrary.'

While she was still smiling I told her that whatever else might be the case I was very happy with the idea of being married to Eugenia Quite. But my pathetic attempt at charm didn't bring anyone much pleasure.

'René, we're hardly married any more. I only agreed to come here to say goodbye. This isn't an attempt at reconciliation. We've tried that. It failed. There's nothing left between us. Believe me, it's over.'

I didn't believe a word of it.

I will stop here for now. Eugenia has just come in.

I met an old gentleman on the beach today. He was walking his dog, a border terrier. His manner was reserved, almost reluctant, but he nevertheless told me a story of a very personal nature. It concerned an old friend of his who had recently died. He spoke slowly and deliberately, weighing each sentence before dispensing it, careful not to give short measure.

The deceased man had been a friend of his since childhood. There had been three of them initially, all equally close. Each had his own function in the group. He himself had been the level-headed one, the boy of good sense who would arbitrate in disputes, smooth over cracks, lead them through difficulties and keep a wary eye on questions of strategy in relation to teachers, parents and other friends who might try to come between them. The recently deceased friend was the most intellectual of the three, brilliant at mathematics and physics, terrific at problem-solving, able to beat anyone in the school at chess, teachers included. He was also a talented musician. In fact he could turn his hand to most things. But this multitude of talents weighed heavily upon him, appearing to bring him more pain than pleasure. It didn't seem to make much difference whether he studied hard or not, he always performed equally well. Perhaps he felt that he did nothing to earn his success, and that the applause he received wasn't really due, and so in a perverse way he went short on praise, the lifeblood of childhood. The same thing happens to pretty girls who are complimented only for qualities they know they have done nothing to deserve.

The third of the three friends was a small pale boy with baby-blond curls. He was unpopular with most of the boys at school on account of his effeminacy, his uncontrolled fits of giggling, and for being physically weak and bad at sports.

I can't remember if the old gentleman told me their names. I shall call the clever boy Hector and the weak boy Alban. The narrator I shall call Percival.

Alban's strong point was difficult to define, though he certainly had one. Without having to speak he could transform the most banal of activities — tea in a cafeteria, say, or an evening spent studying, or a tiring walk through the grey drizzle of some undistinguished afternoon between autumn and winter — into something exciting and special. When Alban was not there, Percival and Hector would sometimes repeat things they had done with Alban and thoroughly enjoyed, only to find that the activity was no longer the same without him. Walking the same path, admiring the same view, sitting in the same room, without Alban's transforming presence Percival and Hector would feel themselves to be walking out of step, standing in the wrong spot, sitting on the wrong chairs.

Blackberries, for instance, picked fresh from the hedge-row, would be too sour, too sweet, too plentiful, or too scarce. Whereas when Alban was there, even if there was only one ripe blackberry to be found it would always turn out to be the tastiest anyone could remember. This superlative berry he would discover every time, as if by magic, although not necessarily without covering himself in scratches first. Having entered the hedgerow in one place he would come bursting out of the brambles some-where else entirely, shouting out wildly and giggling like mad as he ran over to them, tripping over his laces, staggering and finally almost falling at their feet. Then he would split the great swollen berry in two and give them half each. With Alban, life was a sacrament.

Yet at the same time he was perfectly irreverent, untroubled by acts of daring that expressed the richest sense of contempt towards the adult world. In conse-quence he was disliked just as heartily by the teachers as by most of the boys. The teachers at their school, sadists mostly, tried to bully Alban, and would very much have liked the boys to do likewise. But Percival and Hector, who were both popular and physically competent, con-spired to prevent this.

Percival loved Hector and Alban equally, but Hector, he believed, loved Alban the most because he got from him something he couldn't get anywhere else, something he particularly needed.

Hector was in the middle of studying for a scholarship when Alban died. It was pneumonia. Alban had weak lungs and didn't put up much of a struggle. He didn't seem all that bothered about dying and certainly wasn't scared. An early death seemed to suit his sense of absurd-ity, seemed almost to be what he expected of such a world, and he went with a characteristic smirk on his face. His

last act was to write a little 'apologies' note to the boys
and teachers at school, on a flowery card which Percival
had acquired for him.

I would just like to say how sorry you all are.
Alban.

His last words to Percival were 'I do love the colour of
your hair, Percy.' To Hector he simply lifted up his hand
and gave a playful little wave bye-bye.

Percival was distraught at Alban's death, but Hector
showed no emotion. He won his scholarship, which was
to fund an education commensurate with his abilities, and
took his place at his illustrious new school.

For a very long time Percival and Hector saw nothing
of each other. Hector conceived an interest in ancient
civilizations, which he pursued tirelessly to the pinnacles
of erudition. Percival took a job in the civil service. Later,
growing cynical towards public life, he took a job in
industry and became rich. The two friends kept in touch
through Christmas cards and the very occasional, warily
indifferent face-to-face meeting. It wasn't until they had
both retired, and both lost their wives, some fifty years or
so after Alban's death that, as if inspired by the same
impulse, they became great friends again.

Neither Hector nor Percival was very satisfied with
what they had achieved in their lives. Though they had
both acquitted themselves honourably, their professions
had after all been mere occupations, and their ambitions
diversions. They talked a lot together about Alban, whom,
even from the other end of their lifespan, they both

missed, not so much with the emotional longing of a lost love as with the awareness of a concrete absence, such as might follow upon an amputation. They shared the painful knowledge that, whatever they thought or said about their lives, Alban had been lacking.

Towards the end of his life, for the want of any more suitable nursemaid to help him in his last illness, Hector had moved into Percival's house. Consequently Percival had been by Hector's side when he died. He was delirious during his last hours, and seemed to imagine himself to be preparing for some kind of party or social function. He raved, gently and courteously, about his tailcoat needing pressing, his cummerbund being a little threadbare, his garters being overly tight, the taxi being late, and so on. Just before the end, however, he regained his usual clarity, and his final words appeared to be spoken in a state of lucidity. Raising his head from the pillow he looked Percival in the eye, seized him firmly by the wrist, and said, 'Tell them I'm sorry I couldn't be present.' Percival, realizing how close to death his friend now was, and taken aback by the directness of his words, quickly agreed that he would do so. Hearing Percival's answer, Hector lay his head on his pillow and died.

As Percival told me all this, a quiet smile played on his lips. He had clearly been touched by his friend's death and talking of it brought their intimacy back to him. But he was troubled by it too, for he had made a promise to his dying friend that he could not possibly keep. For not only did he not know to whom Hector wished him to communicate his apologies, he was equally at a loss to understand what Hector's words of apology might mean.

I suggested to Percival that the force of the utterance may have been metaphorical. Percival raised an eyebrow and said he didn't see how that helped him at all. A promise was a promise.

It seems that Percival has decided that the best he can do to keep his promise is to tell the story to anyone who will listen. He wasn't at all interested in my ideas about what the story might mean. We had been pacing slowly side by side along the beach as Percival told his tale. But almost as soon as he reached the end he stopped, touched his hat, wished me good day, and walked off in the opposite direction, his wire-haired terrier snuffling along in his tracks.

(she holds me in the palms of her eyes)

What a pleasure it is to tell a story with a clear narrative arc, a tale that makes some kind of sense of its subject, or at least succeeds in being explicit about its mysteries. That's what I call reality. I wish my story was half so well formed.

René Quite, Eugenia tells me, is in his mid-thirties. He married Eugenia when he was twenty-four and she was twenty-two. They were happy together at first, with common interests in all things intellectual and aesthetic, but gradually they grew apart, René becoming ever more deeply entrenched in his intellectual redoubt, while Eugenia became more and more concerned with achieving a perfect unguardedness of expression and response. Eugenia felt that René disapproved of her because she had, and still has, no general morality to speak of, but seizes eagerly at whatever might serve her desire to create. The crisis came when Eugenia decided she wanted to have a child, an idea René Quite simply could not bear. How could he cooperate in the creation of a new life when it was at least arguable that the very best thing anyone could wish for, rationally speaking, was never to have been born at all? Eugenia was horrified by this attitude and felt unable to carry on living with him, whether he consented to having children or not.

It seems the holiday in Scarby-at-Sea was arranged at Quite's request. For him it was to be a last attempt at reconciliation. He believed that their differences would be resolved once Eugenia came to understand his point of view, which he was always willing to reconsider in the light of rational argument. But Eugenia was convinced reconciliation was impossible. She did not want to be reconciled to someone whose rationality gave countenance to such ghastly ideas. For her the meeting was a way of saying goodbye, of tying up the loose ends and drawing a line. With an uncharacteristically romantic impulse, Quite had chosen Scarby for the attempted tryst. They had shared a memorable winter weekend there shortly before they were married, a weekend of cliff-top walks, stormy seas, dark skies, sudden downpours, intoxicated sex and impassioned discussions.

It was hard for me to wheedle all this out of Eugenia. She dislikes speaking to me of personal things. This is because of what she describes as my past brutality. By this she does not mean that I was violent, but that I was warlike when the arts of peace were called for. She says I was permanently at war, that I was at war with life itself.

I have started pretending to be René Quite again. That is to say, I tentatively accept the principle that he and I may share a common history. I have good reason to. I am in love with his wife. She has agreed to stay here in Scarby until I am 'better'. Once I have recovered myself, she will leave me. Because once I have recovered myself she will not like me any more.

Is life right or wrong? René Quite describes life as a panic attack on the part of molecules. What if he is right? What if nothing in the world can truly count as success? What if existence is utterly futile? Does that make it less futile than nonexistence?

I just looked up *futile* in the dictionary. The etymological root is a word meaning something that pours. Well, life is certainly that. It pours and pours and pours. Long may it reign.

Eugenia spends the day painting, on the beach or by the cliffs. I hang around by the sea, watching the waves. I am coming to understand them. They advance towards the shore, raising themselves up as they go. It is sheer willpower. When they see the bulwark of the land draw near they form a razor-edge. Then they lean down and begin slashing wildly at their roots. They are ambitious. They would sever themselves from the gloppy surface of the sea. They would exist outside their element. They succeed only in becoming liquid rubble. A moment later they are gone. But there is something grand in it nonetheless, when an offshore wind lifts the lip of a wave and spins from the spittle a white cloak of spume. All really wondrous things are futile. Stars and suchlike.

I sleep at the bottom of Eugenia's bed, lying perpendicularly across her feet like a hound, a great gangly mutt who knows no greater happiness than to keep warm his mistress's toes. That is as close as we come to sex. That is intimacy enough for me, and Eugenia seems happy too, though she mocks my devotion. The footboard keeps me from rolling off, and as the bed is a wide one I am not uncomfortable. Admittedly my feet protrude a little at one side, and my head at the other, which causes a little stiffness, in the neck and in the ankles. In profile my limp body must make a lugubrious sight, a loving mouth turned down at the corners. But that is how loving mouths are, much of the time, is it not?

Eugenia encourages me to write lies, to sit down and write goddamned, shameless lies. It will do me good, she says. Truth, she believes, is a kind of depression, and literal language an assemblage of clichés, of use only when there is an imperative need to assimilate the disparate, which is much less often than most people imagine. Hot days, for instance, according to Eugenia, are both common ✳ and nonexistent. The general is not general, she says, for it always excludes the particular. Therefore general truths are always false. Only lies come close to reality.

Bought myself a bucket and spade, at last. Red plastic bucket with a vivid yellow handle and integral turrets. Red spoon-sized spade. Eugenia painted a view of the bay, including the ruined castle, while I made castles out of sand. Lots of small, quick sandcastles down by the water's edge, which were swept away in minutes, then one more ambitious construction towards the end of the day.

✻

Physical objects are condensed light, says Eugenia. Then she shrugs, as if the words meant nothing.

Still she holds me in the palms of her eyes.

Eugenia has finally started to believe I am a different person. Not a person with a different spatio-temporal history, but a different person with the same spatio-temporal history. She says I could conceivably be an identical twin, and jokes that I have perhaps been created out of antimatter. If I meet the original René Quite, perhaps I will be absorbed back into him, or he into me. Or perhaps we will implode and form some altogether different particle.

Eugenia now allows me to exist – I mean 'exist' in the special way – for increasingly long periods of time. When we first met she would only allow me to exist for five minutes at a stretch, and even then only out of politeness. Gradually, as I continue to be myself and not the person she knows, she becomes more at ease with me. Soon she may allow me to exist full-time and in all respects. That is what I hope for.

Because when Eugenia doesn't allow me to exist I find it very difficult to amuse myself. I drum my fingers, fret over the newspaper, feel indifferent to the weather, indifferent even to the sea, which is transformed in a moment from a living, talking thing with moods of its own into a cold, insensate, slopping mass. Then, when I am re-admitted to her domain, it comes alive again, whispering its greeting like a waking child.

(and that was that)

All is blown open. All is fractured. My voice resounds in the darkness. The love story is over. Eugenia has gone.

She invited me into her bed. We transposed ourselves from the perpendicular arrangement in which our relationship had flourished into the more conventional parallel arrangement. I lay on top of her, perfectly balanced, no excessive pressure anywhere. We looked at one another through our eyes, desperate to see ourselves seeing. I slipped inside her. We hardly moved. Even breathing seemed too much. After a while we came together, quaking and crying a little as we did so. Then we came apart, the one body shivering into two. And that was that.

Nothing changed immediately. We lay still for a while and then I rolled off her. She fell asleep first. Her slow breath tickled at my neck as I too began to drowse. We slept without stirring.

Next day, all was emptiness. All was drained dry. Her eyes couldn't reach me through the fog of clarity that enveloped us both. When we looked at each other our eyes met in a sort of blind panic, a mutual inability to focus. We had sex again. She went on her hands and knees. I fitted myself in and went about my work. She looked around occasionally to see if it was still me. It wasn't. It wasn't her either. It was just two bodies, two busy corpses. When she had finished, and I had finished, I fell asleep again. Eugenia went off to paint.

I was woken by the chambermaid. I was lying naked in a bright tangle of sheets, illumined by a single band of steely-grey sunlight. She was looking at me from the shadows at the end of the bed. She shouldn't really have been there.

Sex.

I told her I wanted her to take off her knickers and tights and come and sit on my face so that I could lick her clitoris. She told me not to be obscene and began tidying up around me. I said there was nothing obscene about it. She was bending over, dusting the television. I knelt down behind her and lifted up her skirt, a generic brown polyester affair, part of a uniform. Everything about her was uniform; she possessed no distinguishing characteristics, unless they were sexual. Her buttocks were very round, I remember. I rolled back her tights and pulled down her knickers, leaving them in a tangle at her ankles. She had on black shoes, with pointy toes and sharp heels

that hinted at sexual violence. She bent further over and
rested her elbows on the TV set while I examined her
calves, the vulnerable bits behind her knees, her smooth
thighs, her plump arse-cheeks. I examined everything, first
with my eyes, then with my fingers, then with my lips and
tongue. I could discover no correlation between these three
sets of experiences.

I think she must have found my technique a little too
reflective, because after a while she asked me to hurry up.
Grasping a buttock firmly but gently in each hand, much
as though I were handling a stray lamb I pushed my face
into the inexhaustibly fascinating cleft where the twin
moons of the buttocks, the twin trunks of the thighs, and
the great urn of the pelvis are conjoined. Nosing away at
the slippery meniscus of her sex, occasionally pausing to
pluck a pube or a fragment of womb-lining from my
tongue, I succeeded after a while in making her come. She
pulled my face into her, quivering violently. I don't know
how she kept her balance; she must have been resting her
chin on the television. Then she let me go again, let me
breathe again. I could smell the scent of her arse on my
nose, a pleasant, faintly shitty smell that mingled well with
the sharp, fresh smell of her wetness.

I watched as she removed her stockings and shoes and
socks and knickers and jumper and blouse and bra. Then,
without a word of explanation, she proceeded to make a
phone call to the proprietor, asking him to come up to
the room. Then she knelt down on the floor in front of
me and put my cock in her mouth, seeing how much she
could cram in without making herself sick, murmuring

and cooing in a gooey, chocolatey sort of way as she did so. Then she asked me to fuck her from behind. That's what I was doing when the proprietor came in.

What he did next defies all expectation. He took out his cock and smeared it with a dab of Swarfega. Then he pushed it up my arse. This he did in a pleasant and suitably respectful way, and I found my new condition wholly satisfactory. My cock was in the chambermaid, whose quim was now so eager that her sticky wetness was smeared hotly all over her buttocks and my thighs, and the proprietor's cock, which was much bigger than mine (in fact it felt bigger than me, if that is geometrically possible), was buried deep inside my bowels. I felt like a glove puppet, with a glove puppet of my own to play with.

The three of us rippled together like a flag in a freshening breeze. We were shoaling like fish. I moved when he moved, she moved when I moved, he moved when she moved. I can hardly describe just how companionable this state of affairs seemed to me. A truly sociable predicament to find oneself in, and a great relief after the dreadful loneliness of the morning.

We were all three of us squirming our way to some sort of climax, marking out our meandering path with grievous cries, uncouth yelps and lavatorial sighs, when Eugenia entered the room. She was not at all pleased by what she saw. She had about her all the freshness of a morning spent in the open air. Her cheeks were blooming, her hair was brushed by the wind, her eyes were bright and wide and faraway. Everything about her was clothed, in tweeds and other natural, unperverted fabrics. Under her right arm she carried her easel, and in her left her paintbox and folding stool. A sweet smile of greeting curled up and died on her lips. She probably smelt us before she saw us, and by the time I had turned to look her way her eyes were averted. We stank, the three of us, of sweat, semen, blood, hair, urine and tears. Our eyes were unfocused, bleary with sensation, heavy with waking dreams. Our lids were drooping with delight. When the proprietor looked round to see what had caught my attention, he immediately ejaculated. This caused me to ejaculate, which caused the chambermaid to climax too. We popped like three corks.

Eugenia left the room before we could unplug ourselves. I cried for a bit afterwards. The proprietor hugged me and the chambermaid hugged me, but their ministrations served no purpose. I asked them to leave me and curled up alone on the bed, my unsleeping eyes baffled by the continued existence of daylight.

(Brian knows all about truth
and falsehood)

Today I received a call from a colleague at the university asking me whether I was ready to go back and teach. Term starts next week. I told him he had the wrong man. Still no sign of René Quite, though. Maybe he is me after all. Or I him. If so, then there will be one less person in the world. Does it really matter if that person happens to be me?

I have started to drink. I'm in the pub right now, the Ring O' Bells. I'm waiting for my friend, Brian Smith. Brian Smith is a journalist. Not a journalist like me, who gets himself nowhere producing inconsequential verbiage about their identity crisis, without even bothering to note down what day it is, but a proper journalist, who fills up dated pages of newsprint with inconsequential verbiage about current affairs. At least this is what he used to do, until his drinking got out of hand and he told the news editor where to get off. That was his last job on a national paper. Now he works on a local here in Scarby, where he files reports on oversized wedding cakes and writes restaurant reviews of fish-and-chip shops. But this is humiliating and cannot go on for long. He feels he is no longer fulfilling his purpose in life. He was once a top-class investigative reporter, and that was when being an investigative reporter meant something. He still carries a little tape-recorder everywhere with him. He also takes notes in shorthand. When I am drunk I ask Brian to let me look at his shorthand notes. The angular marks remind me of Eugenia's painting.

I have confided my own story to Brian. He is very interested. He thinks it could be big. He thinks a man whose identity has been stolen by a university philosopher could go front-page. I tell him he is only being kind, that my story is hardly of national interest. I tell him it probably isn't even true. Brian knows all about truth and falsehood because in journalism you get sued for getting it wrong. He wants me to sub him enough money to leave his job on the *Scarby Herald*, retrace my steps, locate René Quite, discover how I came to be injured, and settle the question of my identity once and for all. He says my wife sounds like a right little tease. If I look at it his way I can't lose. It probably isn't even my own money I'd be spending.

Brian feels that my story will help him to express a part of himself. He envisages it as a kind of mystery story, possibly serialized over several weeks. Hopefully there will be a crime angle. Who knows, if we are lucky there may even be a political angle to explore. Brian sees it as a classic case of institutionalized iniquity, the little guy fighting against the educational and medical establishments.

Brian is a problem drinker. He has been soaking himself in alcohol for so long now that he has become slightly misshapen, like a sagging brain in a jar of formalin. He wears a black leather jacket and dark trousers which, despite being too small for him, hang off his body formlessly. He has dark curly hair that seems to have been trimmed with a bread knife, and his skin is pocked and red. Red at night, that is. In the mornings it is yellow. He talks without expression. No, that's not right, it's not that he lacks expression, it's that he has too much of it. Or that it's someone else's. Yes, that's what it is. He talks as if his vocal modulations and facial movements were learned from an educational videotape designed for people who were brought up without human contact: Kaspar Hauser's Humanity as a Foreign Concept course.

Brian has been through it. This makes him sympathetic to me, because I'm going through it now. That's why I've taken to the sauce, to assuage my suffering. Brian took to the sauce years ago and it never did him any harm. Ha, ha, ha.

Night after night we sit side by side on a velour bench seat, bobbing forwards for our pints and cigarettes like a pair of strange battery-farmed animals fattening ourselves up for the table. The more you drink the thirstier you get.

Pissing becomes an irritatingly frequent necessity. The pub fills and empties and fills and empties. On Friday and Saturday nights it just fills and fills until it is hard to get to the bar, so Brian insists that we buy rounds of four, six or even eight pints at a time. We drink different types of beer – lager, bitter, mild, stout – but whatever the chosen beer we stick to it religiously, for the sake of our stomachs.

The first hour or two usually goes rather slowly. This is when the hard work is done and the foundation is laid for the rest of the evening. If one lays the foundation well then time soon begins to accelerate. By the time the pub closes it is racing, positively zooming along, moving too quickly even, too quickly to allow so much as a thought to be flung on board, never mind expressed. When time progresses at this speed it can make you dizzy.

Brian continues talking even when we are up to full speed. What he says appears at first to make sense, but one soon learns that he is only repeating stock phrases, probably things he learned on his Humanity course. You can tell this because eventually words start to snap off from the end of his sentences. Then the sentences start to crack apart in the middle too, and the fragments recombine. Later still random mutations occur. For instance, having repeated 'It's all a question of beating the opponent. You and I know who the opponent is. Not everybody knows who the opponent is . . .' a dozen or so times during the course of the evening, he will end up saying something like 'Question the offering . . . Question the offering . . .' over and over, able neither to cough up any new words, nor rearrange the ones he still has on his tongue. He continues to modulate his voice with what passes with him as expression, but the effect is blatantly synthetic.

But then Brian is blatantly synthetic. That, I think, is what I like about him. He was probably organic once, in a former life, but there's nothing left of that now. He was synthesized from the rotten remnants of his old self, together with some odd bits of other people's personalities they discarded in moments of insight. Unseeing and unseen, he talks only to himself. Yes, that's what I like about him. Being with Brian is like being alone without anybody but yourself knowing it. He provides companionable solitude. Here he comes now, grinning at me across the room, like some domestic animal that was reared without conspecifics, and consequently imagines itself to be human.

Last night turned out to be a bit of a blast. I'm covered in cuts and bruises. I can hardly move without setting off a chain reaction of inexplicably linked pains. Some of the links seem physiologically dubious. For instance, when I touch my left earlobe the second toe of my right foot hurts. All this pain has the bizarre effect of making me giggle.

I am thoroughly, deeply ashamed of myself. Which is a relief, because I felt like that anyway, but until last night had nothing definite to hang the emotion on. Now at least the floor of my mind is less cluttered.

As usual, after a few drinks Brian and I fell to discussing my case. He urged me once more to provide him with the money needed to launch a full-scale investigation. Sitting there watching him take my predicament so seriously I was filled with a dreadful feeling that he was nothing more than a figment of my imagination, something I had created in order to lend weight to the illusion that I do not know who I am. He seemed to be saying everything I wanted him to say, to the point where I began to suspect it was I who was operating his lips. As this uncanny conviction intensified, Brian himself became more and more vehemently empathic. We seemed to be collapsing in on one another, not in the manner of two people falling in love, so much as in the way in which two zeros might come together, stay apart, or even breed a third without anyone being any the wiser. That is to say, we would have collapsed in on each other but could not, for there was nothing of either of us left to collapse. There is in my heart a terrible hollow. The blood is pumped round, but that is all that happens there. Brian I doubt even has a heart. His body is stuffed with dirty bits of cellophane, balls of wool, corrugated packaging materials and old clothes.

These schizoid delusions, no doubt the consequence of getting very drunk for the tenth or eleventh night in a row, stimulated in me a great and uncharacteristic desire for action. I reflected on my recent experiences, remembered coming round in the hospital, remembered my early attempts to make sense of my predicament, remembered my evasion of the sanitizing influence of Dr Nous, remembered my determination to do something about the menace of René Quite, remembered Eugenia, who is no longer a person to me, nor a god, but rather a world from which I am forever excluded. I remembered all this and grew angry. At least, I pretended to do so. I suspect I may simply have been bored. Anyhow, a man who was standing at the bar caught my attention. To my eye he looked suspiciously like René Quite. Or perhaps he looked like me. Whatever. So I went up behind him and hit him on the head with a massy glass ashtray. Clonk. I was rather half-hearted about it, though, bringing the thing down sharply at first, but subsequently decelerating it with all my strength, so that it made contact with the back of the man's head with all the force of a polite nudge. Even so, the man didn't look his gift-horse in the mouth, but seized eagerly upon the opportunity to give me what Brian later described as a 'proper panning'. And rightly so.

Brian took photographs with a pocket camera. Apparently he takes it everywhere with him, together with his little tape-recorder and his shorthand notepad. It has a built-in flash. He says he got some pretty good shots. He thinks they might be able to use one on the front page of the *Herald*.

Once my opponent had sated his desire for kicking and punching, the landlord threw us both out onto the pavement. I thought that my thrashing was going to be continued in the street, but my assailant had tired himself and was to some degree placated by his exertions. He and Brian stood chatting together as I gathered my strength and slowly clambered to my feet. Brian told me later he was getting the other man's side of the story. Brian is always scrupulously even-handed.

Later in the evening I agreed to give Brian the money to take a couple of weeks off work and devote himself to researching my story. I cashed a cheque at the hotel. Brian left straight away, promising to send me regular reports letting me know how he was getting on. I found him two hours later, slumped against the railings on the seafront, dead drunk. He slept on the sofa in my room and left again early this morning, taking with him a few bits and pieces belonging to Quite, much like the items one shows to a bloodhound to put it on the scent.

I don't see that it matters much whether I am René Quite or not. Whatever I am, whoever I am, I am not.

(scribbles of blood)

Wandering around town today I witnessed an interesting spectacle. Above the entrance to the Victoria Arcade is a mechanical clock decorated with life-sized figures that appear from little doorways to perform a drama. The story they enact is a kind of variation on a theme from *Punch and Judy*. If I'm passing within a few minutes of a performance I always stop to watch.

The drama, such as it is, goes like this. On the quarter-hour a rather earnest looking mechanical policeman slides surreptitiously from his old-fashioned police box, bends at the knee by way of greeting, then, with a delicate tap of his truncheon, rings the bell that hangs by the door of his box. He has brightly painted eyelashes and rather overdone rouge. All in all he looks rather camp, and if there are any real policemen in the area when their mechanical counterpart appears, they tend to become a little self-conscious, mooching around casting dark looks at passers-by as though selecting someone to arrest. His time-keeping function duly discharged, the mechanical policeman bends at the knee once more before sliding back into his hutch. One last obsequious curtsey and the blue door snaps shut.

The next action takes place on the half-hour. The door to the little butcher's shop opens and a garishly dressed woman of florid complexion appears, all afluster, holding loose in one unthinking hand a string of plump but rather mangy sausages, the exact colour of the bacillus *clostridium botulinum*. She pauses for a moment in the street, trying to decide what her next port of call should be, when a Jack Russell terrier comes flying out of his kennel, grabs the sausages out of her hand, and scurries off with them. I say he comes flying, but actually this part of the show happens terribly slowly, as if an unimaginable quantity of fluff had found its way into the mechanism.

The woman, of course, is speechless. Turning her head this way and that with an owl-like torsional mobility of the neck, she is now stricken by a second bout of indecision as she tries to make her mind up what action to take vis-à-vis her recently departed sausages. After some moments a bowler-hatted gentleman with a belly like a vast lactating breast appears audience-right to ease her predicament. The woman, I shall call her Ada, has no sooner indicated to the man, to whom I shall refer as Neville, the direction in which the dog has fled, than Neville, pausing only to raise his hat to Ada and his eyebrows to the audience, is accelerating off audience-left in hot pursuit of the larcenous canine.

Ada waits patiently outside the butcher's shop until quarter to the hour. It seems her anxiety over the loss of her sausages has caused her to lapse, or perhaps relapse, into a state of reverie bordering on catatonia. Her solitary vigil is finally broken by the reappearance of the policeman, who salutes the woman with a familiar flex of the knees, rings his bell with his truncheon, and is about to return to his crossword puzzle and his brew when Ada jerks awake, stops the policeman in his tracks and, raising her arm in the direction of her departed sausages, her fingers still frozen around the memory of their satisfying mass, informs him silently of the drama that is unfolding.

At this point the policeman's over-earnest look is suddenly rendered appropriate by circumstances. (In this respect, if no other, he might count himself fortunate, there being many people whose facial expressions never do find a satisfactory context.) Even his make-up job now seems peculiarly fitting, producing as it does sympathetic resonances with the appearance of the distressed Ada. They are united as one in their desire to see the sausages restored to their rightful owner. As the policeman leads Ada into his box to take down her particulars, one begins to wonder if Neville, presumably still puffing and panting in pursuit of the wayward terrier, is wasting his breath for nothing.

Resolution, when it comes, comes swiftly. Just before the hour, the policeman and Ada reappear once more. Her anxiety unallayed, Ada swivels her head through an even more disturbingly wide arc than before, a total sweep of something like two hundred degrees. Still she sees nothing. The policeman, demonstrating once again his talent for sympathetic resonance, follows her lead. Their mutual attunement is such that one cannot help but feel that marriage is on the horizon. Laying the matter of the sausages to one side for a moment in order to attend to his other duties, the policeman is in the process of raising his truncheon to sound the hour when Neville reappears audience-left in a violent state of deceleration, apparently just emerging from hyperspace mode. He has lost his bowler hat, but that doesn't matter, because in its place, raised aloft in triumph, he brandishes the stolen sausages. As Neville and Ada's eyes meet beneath the prepared meats, a feast of precisely articulated emotion is served up to the audience, Neville flicking his eyebrows up and down in alternation, left, right, left, right, while Ada shakes her head from side to side sawing the air with her one mobile arm in a manner strongly suggestive of an ugly mental disorder.

Unnecessary motion now ceases, as all available mechanical energy is channelled into a complex series of transactions during the course of which Neville passes the sausages to Ada, Ada passes them to the policeman, Neville does a one-eighty, reverses into position by Ada's side, and offers her his arm. Ada then takes the proffered limb and the policeman rings out the hour, with brio, as Neville and Ada promenade smoothly off audience-right. Just as the couple are about to exit the dog reappears audience-left, catches up with the loving twosome and follows them off at heel. The turning of the hour acknow-ledged in proper form, the policeman raises his sausages to the gods in a gesture of awe and reverence, before slamming back into his hutch with a quick flex of the knees and a valedictory crunch of gears.

It was 3:28 when I happened to be passing the arcade. A larger than usual crowd was gathered beneath the clock, for all was not as it should be. It seems that after ringing the quarter-hour the policeman had failed to return to his hutch, remaining instead by his bell and walloping it over and over with his truncheon. The arcade caretaker had been called. After staring at his misbehaving charge for a minute or two in sheer astonishment, he had gone off and collected a ladder. Placing the ladder carefully below the access hatch, a narrow opening located directly beneath the elaborate gilt clock that forms the centrepiece of the proscenium arch, he climbed up and started his investigation.

By the time I arrived only his legs could be seen. He was wearing cheap black plastic shoes, grey socks and navy-blue polyester trousers. A band of faded brown overall was also visible. His ankles were white and reptilian with a smattering of long, very straight hairs. That's all I could tell about him. He seemed to know what he was doing, though. Rung by rung he edged up the ladder, as more and more of his body was required inside the hatch. In the end his feet left the ladder altogether. Then his legs began to twitch. It wasn't clear whether this was an attempt to regain a foothold on the ladder, or a side-effect of the effort he was putting into freeing whatever part of the mechanism had jammed. The spectators cried out, but any answer the caretaker might have made was lost in the racket the policeman was creating with his bell. Finally, after one especially vigorous twitch of the caretaker's legs, the mechanism burst into new life. But this life was not as it should be. The narrative had mutated.

The first thing that happened was that a butcher appeared from the shop doorway. Yes, a butcher. This wholly new character raised a gasp of surprise from the assembled shoppers. He was slim and virile in appearance, and his face wore a disturbingly cynical sneer. Not even the oldest members of the audience had seen him before, or even heard tell of him. He must have been written out of the script, presumably as a result of mechanical failure, two or even three generations ago.

As a result of his lack of exposure to the sun his colours were brighter than those of any other character, more vivid even than the florid Ada. A bright ginger moustache positively fizzed against his erotically pale and liverish skin tone and full, sanguine lips. His head was covered with a straw boater, cocked at a jaunty angle, with a striped band to match his blue and white apron. The rest of his clothing, shoes included, were brilliant white. His shirtsleeves were rolled up to his biceps, to reveal muscular, hairless forearms. In his right hand he gripped a huge gleaming cleaver and from his left a long steel extended upwards. The moment he emerged he began rubbing the two together with a vigour that made one surprised not to see a shower of sparks. Overall, the impression he made was somewhat supernatural.

The butcher had not been sharpening his cleaver for more than ten seconds when the policeman, suspecting trouble, made a pre-emptive lunge with his truncheon. But the butcher was out of the policeman's reach, and continued sharpening his cleaver willy-nilly, making the policeman look terribly ineffectual. Next, Ada appeared behind the butcher. She seemed distressed. Despite searching frantically this way and that for some means of escape she simply couldn't get out of the shop. Her head was rotating back and forth so fast one could almost imagine she was attempting to make fire with her vertebrae. Moments later the dog appeared from its kennel, sausages in mouth, and whizzed off audience-left. This was the final straw for Ada, and her head now started rotating smoothly and continuously in an anticlockwise direction.

This tableau was held for a couple of minutes: Ada's head spinning at constant speed, the butcher rhythmically sharpening his cleaver, the policeman attempting to subdue him with badly aimed blows. The more public-spirited members of the audience started discussing the possibility of mounting some kind of rescue attempt, for of the caretaker nothing more than his shoes could now be seen. A practical-looking young woman had her foot on the bottom rung of the ladder when her mercy mission was interrupted by a sudden gasp of excitement from the crowd. Neville had appeared audience-left, brandishing the dog at head height. With excellent dramatic instinct, he marked his entrance with a momentary pause, before accelerating audience-right with all the violence of an aircraft-carrier launch mechanism, thrusting the helpless dog square into the butcher's mush, decapitating him instantly.

The head came off clean at the neck and fell a good fifteen feet to the pavement below, clearing a radius in the crowd which it immediately filled with a thousand crumbs of plaster. The butcher's response, at least that of his mortal remains, was to raise his cleaver up to shoulder height and slash out at Neville's head and neck. At the same time, only too pleased to find a wrongdoer within truncheoning distance, the policeman started bludgeoning Neville from behind. Splinters, plaster and paint flew as Neville's head and upper body were gradually eroded by blows. The audience could restrain its laughter no longer.

Abruptly, when the guffawing was at its height, the mechanism stopped. What remained of the laughter ran its trickling course, and then all was still. The first person to move was the forgotten caretaker, who wriggled himself adroitly out of the access hatch until he had a toe-hold on the ladder once more. The young woman held the ladder steady for him as he descended. Children scurried around the pavement picking up splinters, wondering at the withered skin of yellowing paint that covered the descriptive outer surfaces, and how oddly it contrasted with the rough red pine flesh of the newly exposed interior.

When the caretaker finally reached the bottom of his ladder all faces turned his way. The onlookers were aghast at what they saw. For the poor man's scalp, face and hands were covered with scribbles of blood, cuts and gashes which stood out against his ashen complexion with a fleshy brilliance that had all our hearts pounding. The apparently harmless mechanical breakdown we had been witnessing had not lacked a victim after all. This unassuming *deus ex machina*, whose creatures had so faithlessly rebelled, had, in his struggle to retake command, thrust his very body into the mechanism.

Oblivious to his audience, rapt by the sight of the

damage done to his precious marionettes, the caretaker was shedding quiet tears. After a few moments, during which members of the crowd attempted to console him with kind words and gestures, he took down his ladder and retreated to his office. A young woman with three young children lingered behind after the crowd had dispersed, collecting together the fallen splinters. The children filled the woman's two cupped hands with this sacred detritus. She wandered around for a while, searching for someone who might accept her offering. Eventually the elderly man in the lottery booth agreed to take it. He put the bits in the brown paper bag that had contained his lunch, promising to see to it that it was passed on to the right people.

No word from Brian.

(this relationship of intimacy
with a dog)

Walking on the beach today I got talking to a man called Churchwarden. Churchwarden has an extraordinarily obedient dog. He only seems to have to imagine what he wants the dog to do and the dog does it. The dog, which is of some shaggy, white-bearded variety, watches him intently all the while with omniscient green eyes. Churchwarden does not abuse the dog's devotion by asking him to perform silly tricks, however. If anything, their relationship works the other way around. The way they play together is most unusual. Churchwarden picks up a stick, gives it to the dog, and the dog goes racing across the sand with it. The dog then drops the stick, often some distance away, before returning to his master's side. Churchwarden then goes and fetches the stick, bringing it back to where the dog is sitting and dropping it at his feet. And so their game continues.

Churchwarden explained himself by saying that it was he who needed practice in the virtue of obedience, not his dog, who is already perfect. I wonder what he means by saying his dog is perfect? He also told me that his father hated dogs, to the point where, when out walking on the heath near his home one day, he lost control and cursed one violently. I do not understand the significance of this information either.

I cannot stress too strongly how strangely their relationship struck me. When they walk along together side by side, they seem to be competing to see who can walk most obediently at whose heel. As each struggles to remain a respectful distance behind the other, the net effect is that they walk more and more slowly, until in the end they come to a halt in the middle of nowhere, like some absurd religious procession that has taken a wrong turn.

Despite the obscure nature of much of his conversation I found myself enjoying Churchwarden's company greatly. He has thought of everything and has an answer for everything. This is reassuring, even though I have little idea what his answers mean. We spent the morning wandering around town together. He has lived in Scarby all his life and we bumped into many of his acquaintances. He introduced them to me. This was pleasant of him. Since Brian left I have started to feel lonely. The hotel proprietor is still very friendly towards me, but I can't bring myself to speak to him because of the part he played in my downfall. The chambermaid doesn't want to talk to me, in fact she refuses even look at me, but that doesn't bother me unduly. I think she's just making the boundaries clear.

Churchwarden invited many of the people we met to a big dinner party he is throwing on Saturday evening. He has invited me along too. He thinks I will fit into his circle of friends very well.

I told Churchwarden about my personal identity problem. He wasn't the slightest bit perturbed. He said he thought that my situation was much more common than I imagined. He thought that the bang on the head I received had probably caused a bit of physiological amnesia, which I had then built upon to suit my own purposes. He says being yourself is the most difficult thing in the world, and that decreasing numbers of people manage it. Most people, he says, lose track of who they are somewhere between waking up in the morning and opening their eyes. That's why he has a dog.

The dog watches him from morning to night, and wakes him up again at daybreak by licking his face. He says it knows him better than any human being ever has or ever could. He believes it even knows his dreams, though he doesn't explain how this could be the case. He says that his acute sense of his dog's awareness of him, and willingness to accept him as he is, warts and all, makes possible a self-knowledge of unparalleled depth, which is nonetheless charitably inclined. This enables him to be himself to a degree that life without a dog necessarily precludes.

This relationship of intimacy with a dog (or, as he sometimes puts it, a 'true dog') is not only a practical necessity, but also a theoretical requirement, if we are to reach our potential and live at peace with ourselves in a state of hope, rather than suffering the death-in-life of despair, which is how most of us actually live. This is because we are neither created nor continue to exist by virtue of our own will, but are determined and maintained in existence by our dog. The fact that someone might refuse to acknowledge that they have a personal dog does not affect this relationship of dependency, any more than refusing to wear a watch makes a person eternal. On the contrary, it is only once we have acknowledged that we have a dog that we can understand the importance of finding that dog, of owning it and of living with it. For it is only by coming to know our dog that we can come to know ourselves, and come to be ourselves. Whereas, by spurning our dog and living wholly amongst people, we exist only in a fragmentary form, the slaves of partiality.

In short, Churchwarden is convinced that without a dog human beings cannot but lose themselves. So he makes a habit of befriending the dogless and working to convert them. He understands the dogless, because he himself was dogless for years, partly as a result of his father's renunciation of the canine way, and partly because of what he calls his own innate rebelliousness. He told me I should expect to meet many dogless people at his party, all of whom had lost themselves, and all of whom pretend one way or another to have found themselves without owning a dog. But their apparent personal discoveries were nothing but snares, fragments of soul reflected in the broken mirror of our social imagination. Only the beneficent eyes of a true dog could do for them what they hoped, with despairing optimism, to do for themselves.

As I write this I'm struck by the fact that Mr

Churchwarden is a pretty strange type, and that I can make neither head nor tail of what he says. But when I was wandering around town with him, watching him doing tricks for his dog, I have to admit I felt very differently. I felt that he was offering me some kind of solution, and was very attracted to the idea of buying a dog myself. In the course of our wanderings we did in fact pass a pet shop. A black Labrador pup was curled up in a basket in the window. In the past I have always thought of pups and babies and all infant creatures as quintessentially dependent beings, but looking at this Labrador I was overwhelmed by a sense of the dog's independence from humanity, and its almost illimitable inner strength.

It was certainly suffering in its dirty little basket, exposed to the full heat of the midday sun as it was, with neither water nor food to sustain it. But the thing is, the dog was perfectly self-contained in its suffering. Far from whimpering and clawing for attention, it looked at me with proud, compassionate eyes, as if out of the two of us the one most in need of comfort was I. Churchwarden told me briskly that he thought it promising that I was moved, but that it was silly to get upset about the fate of one puppy, when the universe was suffused (I think that was the word he used), suffused with suffering dogs, who wait patiently for their owners to find them, and be saved.

He is an impressive speaker, but I have to say in retrospect I think he is probably insane. Or perhaps I have lost the thread of his argument, which was nothing if not subtle. When he left me to go and feed his dog I spent the rest of the afternoon in the pub, so drink may have caused me to jumble up some of the things he said.

I dare not show my face in the Ring O' Bells any more. I've taken to drinking in the Wise Owl, just around the corner from the hotel. It's a depressing establishment, but I feel very safe in there. Even if I were to attack someone again, I do not think I would come to much harm. The great majority of the Wise Owl's regulars are elderly or disabled.

My smoking is coming on well. I now cannot last more than half an hour without a cigarette. That is to say, I could if I wanted to, but I don't. And if I do, all I can think of is the cigarette I'm going to have as soon as I get the chance, so it's not worth trying. A huge amount of pleasure is concentrated in the tiny actions of removing the cigarette from its packet, lighting the exposed shreds of tobacco, and inhaling. The first two puffs are pure heaven. The smoke penetrates my woolly being like an intimation of immortality. It's a beautiful little sacrament, though in truth it doesn't stretch very far. The trick is to increase one's addiction. That way the sacrament can take place more frequently. But this takes time and application. To be honest, I sometimes simply forget to smoke, and go for up to an hour without lighting up. I have probably started too late in life. Even so, I remain optimistic. I have an image of fitting myself, with all my cares and hopes, into a packet of cigarettes and a flask of strong spirits. It would be a kind of modern miracle.

(Churchwarden's house is an epiphenomenal house)

I can't believe it. Brian has turned up. He came knocking on the door of my hotel room at 6:30 in the morning. He was in a dreadful condition, unshaved and unwashed, with sunken eyes and dirty clothes. I told him he was a poor excuse for a searcher after truth and he burst into tears. He sobbed that the case was proving more difficult to crack than he had anticipated. When I refused to show him any sympathy and told him that I knew very well he had done nothing other than drink the money I had given him, he turned off the tears and tried a different tack. Whipping a tape measure out of his pocket he proceeded to take measurements of my skull and limbs. He then took out his little camera and insisted on scouring my body for distinguishing marks. After he had photographed my moles he attempted to make a pictorial record of my genitals too. At that point I withdrew my cooperation. Brian then left, mumbling something about a 7:30 train he had to catch. I threw on some clothes and accompanied him to the station, making it very clear to him that this time I wanted to see results. I watched him onto the train. As it pulled out of the station he gave me the black power salute.

In the station I picked up a copy of the *Herald*. It contained an article about the Victoria Arcade marionettes. During the course of the débâcle the caretaker lost the top joint of his right index finger. By the time he had discovered the precise part of the mechanism that was causing his narrative to wander so drastically from its expected course, he could already hear the dreadful hacking and bashing that was taking place on stage, and in a desperate move to save what the newspaper described as the thing he most cared for in his work, he plunged his finger between the two errant cogs. The top joint came away with a minimum of pain, jamming neatly between the cogs and arresting the contraption in its perverted trajectory. Experts think that the performing clock can be saved, if money can be found to pay for it. The caretaker says that if this happens, and fresh generations of children are able to enjoy this nineteenth-century delight, then he would think his sacrifice more than worthwhile.

Local historians are engaged in a lively debate concerning the significance of the butcher, and exactly how he would have fitted into the original story. A faultline has opened in the continuum of opinion, separating those who believe that the reconstruction of the original narrative should be left to mechanical engineers, who are qualified to interpret the cogs and levers that determine what dramatic interactions are physically possible, from those who believe that bare causality leaves open many dramatically absurd possibilities, and that mechanically qualified people rarely have a fully developed sensitivity to the less precise but ultimately richer logic of human behaviour. No one, so far as I know, has yet suggested that the narrative conventions of nineteenth-century performing-clock dramas might be the most reliable starting point for a reconstruction.

The caretaker's own view is that objectivity in these matters is neither possible nor desirable, that the butcher was clearly up to no good, that for all we know his maker may well have intended him to remain a part of the back story, that his influence on a young audience is at best untried and at worst corrupting, and that in the light of all these factors, once his head has been replaced, he should be returned to the well-deserved obscurity of his shop. The editor of the *Herald* spoke out against this view, praising the caretaker's brave work in salvaging what he could of the toy, but arguing strongly that nineteenth-century moralizing had no place in a modern shopping centre.

Today is the day of Churchwarden's dinner party. I'm going to buy some clean clothes and get a haircut.

Dead, oh dead, oh dead, oh dead. Dead, oh dead, I killed him. I'll wrap the body in a sheet and put it in the freezer.

It's the shadow of a thing, the merest shadow. Effie will not mind it.

It was a roaring, cursing, castrated lush of a day. The wind was making an embittered assault on all that is stable and solid, exerting every fibre of its makeshift muscle in a jealous attempt to disrupt earth's languor. The sea frothed and spat in sympathy with its insubstantial playmate, building in confidence as the day rattled on, until breakers the height and breadth of Death itself snarled and snapped at the shore. Flora and fauna, those two unlovely scrofulas that erupt and heal, erupt and heal again on earth's disfigured face, clung on like vices at a scourging. I put on my camel-coloured slacks, yellow shirt, puce tank-top and shiny brown brogues and made my way on foot towards Mr Churchwarden's house.

There is an understated opulence about Churchwarden's residence that surpasses any other dwelling I have ever entered. Located high up on the landward side of the hill upon whose crest the ancient castle stands, this Edwardian mansion has the satisfying quality of being comprehensible in outward proportion, while being bewilderingly large and rambling inside. Mr Churchwarden's house contains many homes, for he has invited several of his friends to stay with him, allowing them to carve out nooks for themselves amongst the countless passages and annexes. Once they have been there a few weeks most of these people, unless they are allergic to dogs, find it hard to depart.

The large garden is ornate and highly cultivated. Churchwarden's gardener, Gabble, specializes in plants which have strong graphic qualities. Churchwarden suspects that, like many of the lower mammals, Gabble sees well enough but does not have the benefit of full colour. He thinks this because Gabble's garden contains some of the most painful colour combinations imaginable, as well as some profoundly tedious areas of chromatic uniformity; as for instance the wide border to the right of the path leading up to the front door, which is stocked with plants whose flowers and foliage are, to a sepal, pale yellowy green. Gabble says simply that he is a monochromist, that he sees colours as vividly as any other lunatic, but that his garden is designed to be viewed in the gloaming, or by moonlight, when the necessary evil of direct sunlight packs its bags and slithers off to torment the other side of the globe. It is only then that the true being of what he calls his 'silent ones', by which he means his plants, is allowed to stand forth.

Gabble is a remarkable man. He speaks in a very off-putting fashion, with lots of spitting and gurgling and huffing and sucking, so that the exact content of his utterances is unusually hard to decipher. But when you make the effort, and succeed in extracting the melody from its inharmonious accompaniment, you very often find yourself left with something thoroughly whistleable, which will remain with you for a long while. That's what Churchwarden says, anyway.

The entrance hall is spacious. It has a double-height ceiling and boasts an unusual asymmetrical pair of staircases, both of which lead up to the same first-floor balcony. As you enter the hall, ahead of you and to the right is a wide, elegantly sweeping staircase, trammelled by highly polished mahogany banisters. A little to the left of this a perfectly straight and far narrower flight of stairs mounts steeply and directly to the upper storey. The risers in this staircase are so tall, the treads so far apart, that one's thigh must be lifted to the horizontal with each stride. Any steeper and one could conceivably fall off the top step and hit the floor at the bottom without making contact with the staircase on the way down. Churchwarden told me that the left-hand staircase is designed for those occasions when one has to rush upstairs in a hurry, to retrieve a book perhaps, and would therefore find the decorative extravagance of the long, curved staircase frustrating. He suggested I look upon it as the uphill equivalent of a fireman's pole. A conventional, downwards, fireman's pole is located to the left of the steep steps. Churchwarden had these features installed when he was a younger man, more taken to fits of urgency than he is today.

The steep steps looked dangerous, but Churchwarden insisted that they were not. Because they look dangerous, he says, everybody watches what they are doing when they use them. In fact it is the relatively tame, elegantly sweeping staircase which causes the most accidents. It is so grand and glamorous in appearance that people often become self-conscious when using it, especially when descending into a crowded entrance hall. Self-consciousness causes people to lose their rhythm, and in that way they miss a step, trip up, and end up rolling head over heels to the bottom.

Amy, Churchwarden's anorexic friend, fell down in just this way that very evening. She was suffering not so much from intoxication as from an abiding faintness, the effect of severe and prolonged self-starvation. She broke her leg in the fall, and bumped her head, and squished her nose, transforming it from a well-finished, chiselled creation with arched nostrils and a delicately aquiline bridge, into something that looked more like a sculptor's preliminary smear of purple clay. Even so, all were agreed that the fall might well be a good thing for her. Once admitted to hospital her anorexia would be drawn to the attention of the doctors, who might well be able to persuade her to eat more sensibly while they fixed up her injuries. She certainly wouldn't have agreed to hospitalization under any other conditions. She was a plucky character and would rather die than relinquish control over her physical appearance, especially as she believed herself to be currently coming close to perfection, or at least stretching the leash by which ugliness held her tethered to its maximum extent.

Churchwarden cited Amy to me as a perfect example of what happens to people when they try to live without the objectivity that dog ownership brings. I think he was referring to her anorexia, rather than her accident on the stairs. If one refuses to admit that one's existence is dependent upon one's dog, he intoned, one either slips into the arrogance of laying claim to the authorship of one's own being, or else one throws oneself on the mercy of others, thereby rendering oneself vulnerable to all the fickleness and malevolence of human opinion. One way or another, metaphorically or in fact, in the end all dogless people reduce themselves to mere skeletons, skeletons dressed with a figment of flesh by the impudent fantasies of men.

The floor of the entrance hall is decorated with a disconcertingly ornate mosaic, upon which it is uncommonly difficult to focus your eyes. From this hall, oak doors of every size fan off left and right. The mosaic has the effect of making the floor seem to pulsate, ripple and shimmer, inducing a strong impulse to rush through one of the doors, or directly up the stairs, before seasickness sets in or one simply falls flat on one's face in a state of confused exhaustion. Churchwarden himself, along with some of his more persistent guests, is able to broach the tiles without discomfort. He says this is simply a matter of regular practice, and that even he, after having lived in the house for seventeen years, upon returning from an extended holiday, once fell flat on his face the moment he stepped inside the door.

The opulence of Churchwarden's dwelling is an opulence not of rich materials and thorough craftsmanship, but of human care. One might even call it an opulence of thought. As in a dream, even the absurd and the inexplicable are there for a reason. Emotionally, the overall effect is similar to the pleasing, dull radiance of a stone step worn hollow by human feet. The furnishings and decor are neither of outstanding quality nor even particularly well maintained, but such is the patina of committed cogitation bestowed upon each individual item by the carefully chosen relations in which it stands to every other that even areas of untidiness appear highly wrought.

There is something satisfyingly irreducible about the place. For instance, when you see a chair in Churchwarden's house, you almost invariably want to sit on it. Doors invite you to open them, and the passage or room thus revealed positively begs to be explored. Pot plants demand to be watered. Paintings instil in one a desire to organize an impromptu conference about the artist. Windows insist that one should enjoy their view, if necessary darkening the room first in order to quell unwanted reflections and thus be able to see out into the night more clearly. The copious wooden panelling produces in most people a powerful urge to fondle its mouldings, and absorb the particularity of its colour and grain into memory. Everything is what it is, and does what it does.

Churchwarden tirelessly attempts to give away the heirlooms that inhabit this house of his, saying with sincere offhandedness of whatever he is proposing to make a gift of that he doesn't need it any more, that it is only an old lump of a thing, and that if it would give someone else pleasure he would be pleased – no, delighted – to let them have it. But nobody ever takes him up on his kind offers, and if anyone ever thinks of doing so, it is only for as long as it takes them to shift the object a few inches to the right, or lay hands on it by way of appropriation. For at that moment the thing quickly fulfils Churchwarden's prophecy, and becomes indeed nothing more than a miscellaneous old lump, certainly not worth the effort involved in carrying it away. Then, astonishingly, Churchwarden breezily returns the chair or whatever it might be to its previous position, and it is transformed once again into an object of enviable and significant charm.

Churchwarden's house is an epiphenomenal house. Its splendour depends upon an impalpable set of relations, a mental architecture of cantilevered assonance and alliteration which inheres between the surfaces of things and is apt to disperse and dissolve as abruptly as any iridescent play of light on moving water. In short, the man is a philosopher.

Churchwarden greeted me on the steps of his house. After exchanging pleasantries, I stepped over the threshold to find myself staggering and reeling across the mosaic. Heeling badly to the right, I propelled myself towards the nearest door, through which I stepped with great relief. It opened on to a dimly lit corridor some twenty yards long, at the far end of which was what appeared to be a conservatory, densely packed with glossy fronds and foliage of all kinds. A musty aroma of damp earth drifted my way. I let the door fall shut behind me.

As my irises widened I could make out six wan portals of equal size arrayed along either wall. As I wondered which way to turn, one of the doors swung open and a warm orange glow filled that part of the corridor. I moved towards the light.

The room was small and cosy inside. A hot, dry fire was burning in the grate and a hundred exotic oil lamps and candelabra threw flickering, swaying shadows this way and that, like the setting suns of innumerable continents. In the centre a gaggle of enthusiasts stood hunched over what I could just descry, through the tangle of limbs and craning necks, was the largest atlas I had ever set eyes upon. Its brightly coloured pages were at least the size of the largest folding maps, and in thickness this huge atlas was the equal of four or even five volumes of the *Oxford English Dictionary*. What I had at first thought was the table upon which this magisterial book was resting, I soon realized was in fact a part of the book itself, which was of such unmanageable proportions that it had very sensibly been manufactured with integral legs. The crowd that had gathered around this vast tome consisted of a disparate group of mostly young men and women, whose appearance varied from the self-consciously slovenly to the uninhibitedly spiffing.

That said, in truth I could discern nothing about any one individual, such was the swirling hubbub that enveloped them all, their gesticulating arms, blubbering lips and rattling tongues more attributes of the group than of any one individual. Even so, the personal pronoun was the only word that could clearly be distinguished amidst the ranting.

It took a while, but eventually I figured out what was going on. These people were exchanging travel stories. A page of the atlas was turned, a finger extended to indicate a point on the map, and then ten mouths began blathering monotonously of drunken sprees, strange meetings, inflated taxi fares, unimaginable toilets, breathtaking coincidences, pleasant views, ferocious animals, jungle insurgents, spoiled places, unspoiled places, spoiled people, unspoiled people, unusual food consumed, unconscionable food expelled, exchange rates, air fares, and incredibly cool cultures totally unlike our own. Sentences begun by one mouth were concluded by another. Descriptive gestures made by one person's arm were completed by another's leg. Then, before you could make head or tail of what was being garbled, a fresh page was turned and the whole performance started over again.

I had been watching all this for five or ten minutes when yet another page was turned, yet another finger pointed, but this time the selection was greeted by silence.

An awkward twitching beset the group, then a moment later people began skittering this way and that like chaffinches in a shrubbery, grabbing at the rucksacks and holdalls and thief-proof purses which lay hidden in the shadows of the room. Within two minutes, the room was deserted. Only one young woman remained, delayed by the need to change from her pink ballgown into army pants and a teeshirt. I asked her where everybody was off to. She said she wasn't sure exactly, but that it was a destination in South-East Asia that none of them had visited before. She grinned excitedly at me as she grabbed her leather satchel and fled, leaving the ballgown and pink slippers lying forlorn before the fire.

Finding myself on my own at last I had a look at the atlas. The tortured forms of the great landmasses, the rhizomorphic river systems with their tuberous lakes and inland seas, the filigree divagations of the roads and the strained rationalism of the railway lines, the bizarre and beautiful place names, the visceral undulations of the mountains and the regal monotony of the plains certainly were evocative.

As I pored over page after page of these maps my concentration was disturbed by a noise. One of the chaffinches had returned, and was with difficulty attempting to disburden himself of a rucksack the size, weight and approximate shape of a mummified adolescent. I helped him wrestle his pack to the ground before asking him why he had come back. He sniggered sarcastically and asked me why I did not ask the obvious question. Why had he set off in the first place?

We got talking. He explained to me that he had

devoted fifteen years of his life to travelling the world. He had visited every continent, spending time in more than seventy different countries. He had learned to ask for a room, a beer, the bill, and very little else, in thirty-eight distinct languages. He had collected cultural artefacts by the suitcase load, often not even remembering to mark them with their place of origin before having them shipped back to the place he had once called home. But the truth was he no longer had a home. Every year he belonged less and less to any one place, and had less and less in common with one human being. But now, he declared bitterly, he had had enough, for the error of his ways had become clear to him.

He had left home with the intention of finding himself, of getting straight about who he really was, but all he had done was to lose himself in the confusion. His love of the exotic had been nothing loftier than the love of appearing exotic himself. The pleasure he had taken in exploring foreign places was in truth little more than the relief he felt in evading the questions that faced him at home. Now he feared he had succeeded too far, had succeeded in evading those questions for ever. Now he had become a citizen of the world – which is to say, of nowhere – his own people and culture seemed as bizarre and alien to him as any tribe of jungle-dwelling cannibals. Even his enjoyment of the cut and thrust of travelling now seemed to him a tacit admission that he was incapable of acting as the protagonist in his own life, unless chance first provided him with an arbitrary antagonist, such as want of food, lodging or liberty.

His tirade of self-abuse over, the tired tourist sank into

an armchair and, holding his bowed head in one hand, confessed to me that he felt like a clichéd idea badly translated by a dishonest taxi driver with the help of an out-of-date and probably inaccurate phrase book. Then he started to sob. I tried to comfort him, suggesting that he must at least have a great store of fascinating experiences to draw on. I told him to try not to judge his past actions according to his present state of knowledge, since more than likely the latter depended for its existence on the former. I reminded him that he still had his health and his looks.

My flow of homely consolations was halted when I noticed Churchwarden standing at the door. He signalled for me to come away. When we were out in the corridor Churchwarden urged me not to provide comfort for his guest, since it was only by looking his despair in the face that he had any hope of settling down and getting a dog. Churchwarden glanced down at his own dog adoringly as he said this. The dog returned his look. Still, I felt dubious about leaving the young man in such a state of anguish.

Churchwarden noticed my uncertainty and, as if to demonstrate the soundness of his proposition to me, scuttled off to the conservatory. He returned carrying a hoop, which he proceeded to jump through several times while his dog looked on. Then, standing on one leg while hula-ing the hoop about his surprisingly supple waist, he started reciting from memory the first act of *King Lear* in a high-speed mumble. Cordelia's part he spoke with particular vividness. His dog's eyes never left him for a moment, and I have to admit that I did feel a little envy, hoping that the dog would turn its glance my way, at least for a moment.

When Churchwarden had finished his trick he departed, entreating me to try any of the other rooms in the corridor. Dinner would not be ready for a while yet, but he was certain I would find plenty to do in the meantime. As he left the corridor I noticed that, like Leonardo da Vinci's handwriting, Churchwarden's dog went backwards. I was perplexed that I had not noticed this before.

Feeling the need of a spell of solitude in order to absorb all I had experienced so far, I went for a wander around the conservatory. When I had tired of examining the plants and sampling the cloying odours of their many frantic blooms, I selected another door at random, knocked on it, and without waiting for a reply went straight in.

It was the drugs room. Not something I had expected to find at a party thrown by a man of Churchwarden's age. But then no one could accuse Churchwarden of shallow conformism. In one corner, heroin users lay supine, prone and variously sprawled on the carpet like inconclusive suicides, their syringes and soot-blackened spoons scattered about them. In the centre of the room a couple of amphetamine freaks were playing a manic game of chess, in which move followed move so quickly that the players' hands sometimes collided above the table, and it appeared for a moment that they were playing not at chess but at knuckles. They passed a joint back and forth between them as they played, sucking in the soothing cannabis smoke in a desperate effort to assuage their frayed nerves. Even so, their knees bounced up and down, their teeth grated together, their fingers tapped and their heads nodded and twitched neurotically.

On a sofa to one side of the chess players two women, apparently on Ecstasy, were touching each other's hair and skin, hugging and stroking and smiling at each other, their excited eyes wide with wonder. On the floor at their feet a slim young girl was bingeing on chocolate and sliced white bread. Over by the window a short, squat Asian man was having an argument with an aspidistra. He appeared to be trying to lecture it on politics, and was frustrated because the aspidistra only wanted to dance. A man seated at a glass card-table, on which were arrayed half a dozen freshly cut lines of fine white powder, was taking a break from his mammoth snorting session to address someone, themselves conveniently seated in the farthest corner of the room, on the subject of his startling personal achievements and his equally brilliant future prospects.

Watching all these chemical experiments in progress reminded me that I had had neither a cigarette nor a drink since leaving the hotel. My body was tense, my nerves stripped bare and my mood low. Now I knew why. I lit up. Grateful though I was for the opportunity to smoke, I decided to remain in the room only for as long as it would take me to finish my cigarette. There didn't appear to be any alcohol there, and I found the atmosphere somewhat depressing. Finding a free spot on the floor next to a man on an exercise bike, I sat down and smoked my cigarette, making no attempt to socialize. This wasn't difficult. Apart from the two fumbling Ecstasy highs, the debate with the aspidistra and the cocaine bragging session, no communication of any sort was going on in the room.

I watched the man on the exercise bike out of the corner of my eye. His face was red, his breathing short and his whole body cried salt tears as he chased his endorphin high. He was peddling frantically. He might have been attempting to escape an execution squad. The effect was nightmarish, like watching a giant hamster on its exercise wheel. In fact the whole room resembled some vast cage in which the eager youngsters of a race of giant rodents kept their cute, hairy-headed little humans, watching them breed, fester and go slowly insane, in order to learn about sex and death, and the responsibilities one rodent has to another.

As I was approaching the end of my cigarette, and wondering whether I could smoke another without making myself feel ill, I was joined on the floor by a woman in her thirties. She rattled slightly as she sat down and I recognized the sound of pills bouncing around in plastic pharmacist's bottles. She asked me how I was feeling. I said I was feeling fine, thank you very much. I asked her how she was, but she didn't answer, instead telling me that 'fine' wasn't a good answer because it betrayed a lack of awareness of my deeper mood. Like the rest of the amateur druggies in this place, she said, I clearly didn't understand the elementary principles of psychotropic drug use. I suggested that if she had time to spare she should feel free to enlighten me.

The woman told me that while many of the people in the room had displaced deeper and more challenging desires on to easily quenched psycho-physical cravings, in this way ceding control of their minds, their moods and even their physical health, the real point of doing drugs is the exact opposite of this. Drugs are a way of taking control over your mind and your mood, liberating yourself from the arbitrary interference of actuality. Interacting with the world, in her view, is only a long-winded way of producing psychological effects, such as insight, ecstasy, excitement, aesthetic pleasure, confidence and so on. What's the point in struggling to achieve an actual live sporting victory, or a real-time love affair with genuine bodily fluids, or taking a train to some particular point on the space-time continuum in order to spend a mellow afternoon in some geographically genuine river meadow, when the thrill of success, the intoxication of love, and the aesthetic reverence of nature could all be had out of a bottle, possibly even one after the other during the same afternoon?

She draws an analogy between real-time actual-space humanity, and humanity in its hunter-gatherer stage. Our future counterpart, which she calls the virtual human, she compares to humanity after the domestication of animals and the introduction of agriculture. At present, despite our technological prowess, we are reduced to hunting and gathering our psychological necessities from the wild. Excitement, love, sensual pleasure, we experience as we find them. But hunting is risky, time-consuming and inefficient. That is why, in this richest of all human societies, many people are psychologically malnourished, even starving. Most people simply have no time to go hunting for sensations and gathering emotions. And those who do have time find that stocks are severely depleted. The answer, of course, is to turn from hunting and gathering to domestication and agriculture. In other words, sensations and emotions should be produced in factories.

Due to institutional prejudice against psychotropic drug use, development work on so-called recreational drugs has been severely retarded. This reaction is typical of the way elites have always responded to technological developments that bring pleasure to the masses and threaten to erode their own relative advantages. But in future, proper levels of investment combined with advancing computer technology will enable us to recreate the best experiences of the most exciting, successful, adventurous, challenging and well-balanced lives, without ever venturing further than the local pharmacy. In other words, with one hypo-allergenic capsule and 100Mb of free disk space, the classic first ascent of Annapurna could be yours, amputations and all. Except that, unlike the original climbers, you'll get your fingers and toes back afterwards.

I attacked this woman's position by employing an argument I remembered reading in Quite's notebooks. The argument runs, *If Johnny expresses a desire for a crisp, fresh Cox's Orange Pippin, and I take his appetite away by punching him in the belly, does that mean I've satisfied Johnny's desire for an apple?* The answer, of course, is no. By analogy, I argued, a life of computer graphics and designer chemical stimulation is unlikely to satisfy anyone's desire for human happiness, though it may well take it away.

The woman squinted at me. I don't think she could follow my point. She was a better talker than a listener. Possibly her brain was addled by excessive indulgence in narcotics. Either way, after hesitating for a few moments, apparently reflecting on my argument, she responded by offering me a small blue pill. If I took one of these, she told me confidently, I would certainly feel differently about the whole thing.

Since I had won the argument so far, I thought it would be mean-spirited to refuse to cooperate with her suggestion. So I took the blue pill, her chemical riposte to my more traditional, logical argument, and downed it, together with the half tumbler of vodka she recommended as the ideal accompaniment. She was right – the blue pill made me feel very different.

(the aspidistra licked its lips)

The next person who came up to talk to me was René Quite. I was pleased to make his acquaintance at last, after having read so many of his private and professional jottings. As I expected, he didn't look at all like me. He was just as ugly as I am, but in a different way. My features are organized around a look of baffled curiosity, the sort of look one might expect to see on the face of a hungry man who is attempting to decipher a restaurant menu written in an unfamiliar tongue. Quite's features, on the other hand, are knotted into a grotesque look of certainty. This is the case even though it became clear from our conversation that he is in fact certain of nothing – nothing that is beyond the basic principles of logic, and the utter dissimilarity of truth and falsehood. *Either p or not p*, he cried out gleefully at one point in our discussion. I almost went for his throat. What an absurd belief. He is, in short, absolutely certain of his method, but nothing else. His conclusions he described as being permanently provisional, like all scientific conclusions.

He believes that there is a great question hanging over all human life. That question can be expressed in many different ways. Its simplest form is *What should I do for the best?* Historically it arose the moment human societies became sufficiently wealthy and sufficiently complex to allow people a choice about how to live, and therefore about how to think. This epoch in the history of mankind he calls the Age of Theory. Before all else, he says, man is the theoretical animal. The word *theory*, he told me, is derived from a Greek word meaning sight. Since the dawn of the Age of Theory human beings have not been able to avoid taking a view of the world, and that view conditions everything they do. Unless it's the other way around, of course. In Quite's opinion, because Philosophy tests theories rationally, it is and always will be Queen of the Sciences.

Many people are sensitive to this question, he says, and many attempt to formulate it. But much intellectual activity is a perversion of the desire to answer it and ultimately leads nowhere, though it may be beautiful and fascinating in itself. Physics, mathematics, evolutionary theory and so on have all contributed to our knowledge, but only philosophy cultivates the analytical machinery necessary to resolve in an authoritative way the question of how we should live our lives and what we should strive for. The huge practical benefits of lucubratory endeavours such as medicine and biochemistry he has the temerity to write off as marginal compared to the potential good and ill that can be effected by the answer one makes to the question of what man's place in the world is, and how he should comport himself.

Truculently, and somewhat dishonestly, I presented myself as a satisfied pig who could only be affected to my detriment by engaging in his analytical escapades. He responded by insisting that the better-a-pig-satisfied-than-Socrates-dissatisfied debate was deeply impertinent to both pigs and people, for ultimately neither can choose their natures. Heraclitus pre-empted the whole debate when he pointed out that donkeys preferred rubbish to gold because food was pleasing to them and gold indifferent. I stiffened. Suddenly I was seething. Heraclitus was the only philosopher whom I had ever esteemed. To find myself on the wrong end of a quotation from the great Ephesian, delivered by this outmoded Enlightenment hysteric, was more than I could bear.

He continued talking. People who dismiss philosophers as quibblers are only registering their unwillingness to have their own opinions put to the test. We are all of us philosophers, just as we are all of us singers and all of us dancers. Only our degree of training and ability varies. But none of us is a pig, however much we might try to effect a conversion. A peculiarly modern form of alchemy, when you think of it, he quipped smugly, nodding towards my cigarettes. No, he continued, though the convention of exempting ourselves of responsibility on the grounds of lack of specialism has caught on like wildfire in the modern world, few people are truly convinced by it. That's why disorders of the self are so common. We are most of us disgusted by ourselves and would do anything to be allowed not to look.

Here he fell silent, looking at his feet with a slight air of dissatisfaction. Now it was my turn to speak.

'I thought it was well known,' I said as casually as I could, 'that Heraclitus compared human opinions to children's toys. Hardly an authority for your Age of Theory idea.'

'When he said that,' Quite burst back, 'he was articulating the same perspectivism he expressed when he wrote that a mortal is called dumb by a god as a child is by a man and that alongside a god, the wisest man appears an ape, in wisdom, in beauty, and in all other things. But nevertheless, lovers of wisdom should inquire into many things.'

'Much learning does not teach sense, or it would have taught Hesiod and Pythagoras,' I countered.

'The water of the sea,' whined Quite, with questionable relevance, 'is very pure and very foul. Fish thrive on it, men are poisoned by it.'

'War is universal. Conflict is the rule. The world is bred of conflict,' I yelled. Then I yelled it again, louder and more slowly.

'Sickness makes health sweet and good, hunger plenty, weariness rest,' came the reply.

'What is that supposed to mean?' I demanded, detecting a subtle insult.

'It means, yes, the craving for justice would not exist, were it not that conflict is endemic in human society. But that does not mean that craving can be dismissed, any more than the desire for health can be dismissed, as a mere symptom of illness, and therefore erroneous.'

'Go fuck yourself, you smug wanker,' I responded, and followed up the dialectical point with a good old-fashioned smack in the chops. *Crack.* It felt good. Mr So-called René Quite staggered and fell. Good. Still on the floor, nursing a split lip, he told me patronizingly that he would not hit me back because although he was not afraid of me, neither did he believe that physical conflict between us would be profitable to him. So saying, he moved away, walking crabwise on his hands and knees. The movement of his legs was awkward and comical, somehow reminiscent of a pantomime horse. And at the same time, the sequence in which he moved his arms and legs seemed to be signifying something. What it was I could not at first interpret. Then I realized he was delivering the ugliest, darkest insult yet formulated by the filthy mind of man. And he was doing it by a form of semaphore that he had the audacity to have invented on the spot, specifically for the purpose.

I glanced around the room. Everyone was watching attentively, glancing from my slanderer to myself and back again, checking whether this abominable description rang true. Judging by how absorbed these spectators were they must have thought the characterization spot-on. Then I realized that far from simply being engaged in broadcasting a cryptic defamation of my person and character, he was at the same time prescribing ways in which my outer appearance should be transformed in order that the wretch within should be more accurately displayed on my now malleable flesh.

I held a hand up to my face and felt my nose beginning to swell. The nostrils were dilating beneath my fingertips, the nostril hair thickening and growing spiny. If I was to stop this drastic remodelling of my physiognomy I had to act fast.

I flung myself upon my assailant and held him tight around the chest. Turning him onto his back, the position in which crabs are at their most helpless, I sat astride his belly, pinned down his numerous arms and legs, and landed a sequence of highly effective headbutts on his ugly face. Blood, bone and fragments of cold, grey carapace flew this way and that. Soon I found I had transformed René Quite into a highly decorative fountain of brightly coloured gore. Gradually my anger subsided, and the geyser of anatomical fragments fell back too. Finally, keen not to get a reputation for myself as someone who prefers brute force to intelligent debate, I stopped beating him in order to tell him more precisely what I objected to in his 'Age of Theory' theory.

I was just about to inform him that if he didn't like modern society he ought to go and live in the rainforest with the primitives and see how he liked it, that as far I was concerned theoretical thought was nothing more than sadomasochistic onanism, and that the best thing that could be done with his great question was to set it to music and sing it in the bath, when I was prevented from uttering this inebriated drivel by a multitude of warm, dry hands which reached down from nowhere, lifted me up in the air and transported me to the other side of the room. Anxious voices insisted that I should calm myself. The aspidistra licked its lips with its long, green tongue and winked lasciviously at me. Weak with emotion, and unable to think of any better way of occupying myself, I elected to collapse in a heap and fall unconscious.

(only thirty-two different plots)

When I came round I immediately felt myself to be in a different part of the house. The storm had not been noticeable on the ground floor, but here the agitated air shook the windows in their frames, cooed down the chimneys, and groaned in the roof space above my head. I was surprised to find myself completely naked. It seemed I had been undressed and placed in an oak four-poster feather bed with a pale silk canopy and covers. I couldn't see what colour the silk was exactly, because everything in the room was basted in the thick orange glow emanating from a night-light that stood on the bedside table. I lay very still. I was aware that the blue tablet had taken me out of myself and was unsure whether its effect had yet worn off.

In my mind I reconstructed my encounter with René Quite. Could it really have been him I had been talking to? I desperately wanted to believe that it was. Meeting him had been a great relief. He was exactly how I had always imagined him, mainly in that he was not me. But I was aware of having known my interlocutor's identity with a preternatural certainty that now led me to suspect that I was in fact hallucinating, probably as a result of the drug I had taken. My heart beat a little faster. This meant that more likely than not I had attacked an innocent bystander.

I felt terrible. I had to find the person and apologize, and apologize to Churchwarden too. Then I would leave the party and pray that the police would not get involved. I sat up in bed and started looking around for my clothes. Before I could find them there was a timid knock at the door. I didn't speak, feeling too embarrassed by my monstrous behaviour to declare my presence. The door opened and a pretty young woman let herself in, closing the door quietly behind her, evidently in an effort not to disturb me. When she turned she was surprised to see that I was awake and sitting up in bed.

This unknown woman was touchingly, inexplicably, gloriously concerned about my welfare. It was she, she explained, who had undressed me and put me to bed. I thanked her for her kindness and, after recounting to her what I remembered of my actions, asked shamefacedly after the victim of my assault. The woman sat down on the edge of my bed and informed me delicately that the folding sofa bed I had taken such a strong dislike to was recovering well and had no intention of pressing charges. I was almost as embarrassed as I was relieved to hear what

an idiot I had made of myself. It seems that after talking
in tongues to a drab velour pouffe for fifteen minutes I
had all of a sudden thrown myself upon it, fists flying.
Eventually the pouffe had rolled out of my grasp. I
responded by leaping astride a nearby sofa and pounding
it over and over with my head, until my face was bloody
and I was pulled off for my own safety.

The woman was smiling as she told me all this, and
her eyes flashed with good-humoured irony. She looked
very pretty in the comfortable gloom of the bedroom. I
was astonished by how effectively she made light of my
actions, poking fun at me while at the same time somehow
protecting me from humiliation. Every now and then her
long auburn hair fell over her eyes, forcing her to brush it
back behind an ear or over the top of her head. This
unselfconscious action had the dramatic effect of drawing
back the curtains on her beauty so it could be viewed
afresh all over again. Each time this happened she would
once again take my eyes into her liquid gaze. Then, as her
hair once again began to obscure her face and partially
conceal her eyes from mine, and mine from hers, I felt as
though I were being permitted, entreated almost, to allow
my eyes to wander over her white neck, her narrow
shoulders, her bare arms, her slim thighs. She was wearing
a pullover with the sleeves pushed up. It was made of
some woolly, fluffy fabric that emphasized the delicacy of
her translucent skin.

For all her generosity there was a kind of entreaty in
this woman's attitude, some obscure need that called out to
me. I too felt needy. Apart from craving reassurance that,
despite my outburst of violent stupidity, I was not an

utterly repulsive and laughable figure, I was, I suppose, still suffering from the loss of Eugenia. The truth is I had never for a moment stopped suffering from that loss. The pain of rejection, the dissatisfaction with myself, the emptiness, and the sense of exclusion had all become a part of my life. And now, as I sat naked and vulnerable between silk sheets, I felt that I were being gently massaged by this woman's eyes and voice, and that she was inviting me to relax into the warm embrace of her physical presence.

Each flashing glance from her eyes seemed to contain a new revelation of her need, of her vulnerability, provoking me to open out further myself. Everything I said and did seemed to confirm in her mind some increasingly ardent conclusion, the meaning of which for a while I dared not guess at. We talked of this and that, with shared seriousness where seriousness was due, and common levity when a lighter touch was called for.

Her name, she told me, was Cathy. The sharp spring of the initial *ca–* sound, the soft embrace of the neutralizing *–th–*, followed by the lingering caress of the sweet *–ee* seemed to conjure her very presence. Once I had learned it I used it whenever I could.

Eventually, after the first awkward pause in a conversation that had ebbed and flowed without interruption for at least half an hour, Cathy told me that the drug the narcotics woman had given me was a concoction that combined a mild hallucinogenic with a powerful but short-acting US Army truth drug. Both, she assured me in a low, almost pleading voice, would have worn off by now, and I had nothing to fear about the reality of what was happening between the two of us. As Cathy said this she lifted her hair out of her face, this time with both hands, exposing to my gaze her fine forehead, her delicate ears (that had until now nestled like pale wild flowers in the undergrowth of her hair), and the softest, loveliest parts of her neck. There are no names for such curves, only sighs. At the same time she gave me a look of such candid warmth that I felt as though she were at that moment handing me the keys to her most intimate soul.

I wanted to reach over and embrace her, to pull her head to my shoulder and comfort her with murmured words, heartfelt promises, swift tendernesses and irrevocable confessions of faith. But instead I stayed exactly where I was. I stayed where I was because I knew I did not need to do any of those things. I knew that she was already aware of how I felt, already knew what I was thinking. I knew she knew because when she let her hair fall over her face once again, leaving only her soft lips and one porcelain cheek exposed to sight, she spoke to me, and it was I who was speaking too. My most secret thoughts were given life by her breath. I felt her sweet lips touch the membrane of my soul and I wondered if my life would ever be the same again.

'Something extraordinary is happening between us. Something neither of us has ever experienced before. I feel as though you were talking through me. I feel as though you were already inside me, as though we two had already become one. I have sometimes heard people talk of meeting their soulmate. Well, what a tame experience that must be compared to what is happening now. I do not find my soulmate in you. In you I find my soul. I didn't even know I had lost you. And yet, here you are.

'I want to say, before the next thing happens, as we both know it must, that whatever else follows, whatever filthy crushing circumstances life deals us, this moment will never stop meaning what it means now.'

Who was speaking? Was it her or was it me? It was from her lips the words emerged, but the thoughts and feelings were common to us both. I pulled back the covers of the bed a little. In answer to this unspoken request Cathy stood up. In less than a moment she had shed her clothes and was standing before me in the dim light, allowing me, begging me even, to take pleasure in the unadorned beauty of her strong, slim body. When she sensed that I could no longer restrain myself from touching her, she slipped beneath the sheets, pulling herself close to me with an involuntary shiver.

We made love slowly. I choose not to say sex because, although we experienced a new world of sensual pleasures of the most exquisite rarity, these physical sensations were mere tokens in our souls' colloquy, tokens as intrinsically insignificant as is the physical fact of money compared to what it can buy. For what interested us were the soul's deepest intimacies, the miracle cure that happens when one is taken whole into another's aching heart and held there in a fluttering, wing-like embrace. Such tenderness, such whispered caresses called out all the fragility we were capable of, and when we finally abandoned ourselves to the depths of this terrifying, blinding consummation we thought our souls would burst, so wholly did we give ourselves, each to the other.

Afterwards we lay still in each other's arms, unable to find words to match the wordless conversation we had just shared. Then Cathy went to the bathroom to clean up.

When she returned I saw she had pinned back her hair and taken off some of the make-up that had been disturbed by my kisses. Her manner had changed slightly too. She seemed somehow to be addressing me more directly now, to be revealing more of herself and yet at the same time concealing more too. She had become (how can I put it?) broader but shallower, and I felt my own artesian depths becoming clogged also, through lack of proper maintenance. She dressed with her back to me. When she was fully clothed she went to the door and put the main light on, a crudely vigorous fluorescent with a slightly green cast. It became apparent that the room we were in was used as a store room. Apart from the great oaken bed, it contained only dusty, rubbishy, plasticky things. Cathy looked at me hesitantly across the room before coming over to the bed and sitting down beside me, a little further away than before. This time, as she spoke to me she looked into my eyes unwaveringly, turning away discreetly only when she doubted my ability to control myself. Her hands, I noticed, were folded neatly on her lap in a gesture of finality.

'I'm sorry about this, that was lovely and everything, I mean really, really special, but I don't want you to get the wrong impression. I'm not in love with you and I don't think I ever could be. No, I'm sure I couldn't. Men fall in love with me a lot, and I fall in love with them a lot too, but I suppose what I'm saying is that for me this isn't one of those times. It was very special, you were really sweet, but I don't think we should see each other for a while, and when we do see each other, I think it'll be just as friends. You're a lovely man...' Here she stopped short, realizing that she didn't know my name. I told her I was probably called René Quite.

She gave me a cock-eyed look. 'I thought René Quite was the man you were attacking in your hallucination?' I told her he was. 'You're a weird man, René Quite. You're a lovely man too, but what I'm saying is, no. Not now, probably not any time.'

Needless to say I was astonished by this sudden change in Cathy's attitude towards me. I was astonished that she could be so confident of my vast desire for her, at the same time as denying those very same feelings in herself. I decided to play her at her own game.

'Don't go on, Cathy. Don't feel bad. Because I'm pleased by what you're telling me. This could never have meant anything to me. The thing is, I'm married. I only hope I didn't mislead you.'

Without pausing for breath, Cathy went one better. 'You didn't mislead me. I misled you. I'm dreadful, I'm always doing this, I can't seem to help myself. I do it all the time. And that little speech I made to you, it's incredible, but I must have used that about fifteen times in the last year alone. Not word for word, of course, but basically the same speech. I'm terrible. I'm really grateful to you for being reasonable about it and not getting all wounded and bitter like most men do. You're being really grown-up about it. I mean, of course you are, you're a lot older than most of the men I go with...'

I winced. She had won. I couldn't compete. I lay there, naked, foolish, and old, listening to her dismantle, brick by brick, the enchantment that I had just experienced, turning my gold back into lead with every well-chosen phrase. By the time she had finished, all that remained of our mutual intoxication was the damp patch in the bed, which I could feel cooling against my left buttock.

She gave me a big, sloppy, patronizing, grandmotherly kiss on the lips before she went, being by then so confident of the damage she had done to my beautiful illusions that she had repented and decided that if I wanted we could be friends right away, without first observing her statutory cooling-off period. I was only surprised she wasn't asking me to help her fix her car. I was conquered; conquered and destroyed.

Strangely enough, I didn't give a damn. If what had just occurred between us proved beyond all reasonable doubt that I was hollow as a Halloween pumpkin, that could hardly make me any more ghoulish than I already felt. This temporary phantasm of light had made a pleasant change from the bituminous murk to which I had grown used, and this whole episode could be legitimately regarded as a holiday. No shame in succumbing to the characteristic illusions of a tourist town. Bravo, Cathy, I muttered to myself.

I dressed and made the bed, being careful to pick the pubic hairs off the sheets and pillows before leaving the room. I almost saved one as a souvenir, but wasn't sure which were hers.

To my surprise Churchwarden wasn't waiting outside for me. I had expected him to appear and explain to me how a dog-lover would have avoided the debasing charade of such an ersatz love encounter. I was pleased to be spared the trouble of listening. Feeling low I traipsed along the long, narrow corridor, determined to do what I should have done on my first arrival: locate the drinks cabinet and stick with it until the bitter end.

I followed the corridor along to the balcony that circled the entrance hall at first-floor level. Down in the hallway Churchwarden was opening the front door, greeting still more guests. I reckoned that in my somewhat weakened condition I would be unlikely to be able to cope with the mind-bending mosaic for more than a few seconds, so I waited on the landing until the hallway was clear, intending to swoop down on Churchwarden the moment he was free and demand refreshment. Several couples were arriving fresh from a major shopping expedition. They were overloaded with shopping bags, mostly of the glossy paper kind with rope handles that are favoured by smart boutiques. Staggering like determined drunks in the bar of a sinking ship, they passed off one by one to a door on the right-hand side of the hall. When Churchwarden was alone I made my move, descending the staircase and negotiating the quivering surface of the hallway without incident. I collared him just as he was turning to go. By standing very close to him and keeping my eyes averted from the floor, I found I could stand still without too much difficulty.

My host greeted me warmly and asked after my health. He had heard about my run-in with the sofa, and hoped I was none the worse for it. I wished him the same for his sofa. He could see that I was surprised by his lack of censoriousness. I should realize, he confided, that true dog-owners are seldom reproachful types. Whatever smut or blemish they detect in other people, the good dog-owner will know is his too, at least in potentiality. I was going to take this as my cue to tell Churchwarden (that's odd, I almost said Spacewarden) that I was keen to access his supply of alcoholic beverages and drink myself stupid, when the doorbell rang. Churchwarden excused himself and went to open it.

Turning to face the door would have meant exposing myself to a dangerously wide stretch of mosaic, so instead I continued looking towards the oak-panelled wall. I was waiting patiently for Churchwarden to finish receiving his new guest and return his attentions to me, when I became aware of a familiar voice. I spun around. There, to my amazement, standing only paces from me, was Eugenia. For a moment I thought I must be hallucinating again. Like Hamlet before the ghost of his father, I took half a step forward. Eugenia turned towards me. Our eyes met in the middle of the hall and joined in a little dance, a little jig of fear and pleasure, of terror and of joy, that held in its meticulous and elaborate footwork the possibility of reconciliation. Churchwarden continued talking for a few moments before he noticed that Eugenia wasn't taking any notice of him. Turning to see what had caught her attention, he looked first at me, then back at Eugenia, then stepped to one side to allow Eugenia to enter. She approached me without once breaking off her gaze. We fell into an embrace.

'I'm so sorry, René,' she said simply. 'I've worked it out now. I know why you did what you did. Will you have me back?'

'Now and always,' I replied.

*

Eugenia's car had broken down near Churchwarden's house. She knocked on his door by chance to ask if she could use the phone. She was on her way to the Grand Hotel at the time, to look for me. Churchwarden asked her to stay for supper but she declined, saying she would wait only until her emergency mechanic arrived. Then Churchwarden left us alone. We sat together on a bench seat in the hallway. Eugenia was fascinated by the elaborate symmetries of the mosaic. It seemed I had started to become used to it, because I was now able to look down without discomfort or dizziness.

We discussed the patterns for some time. The vertiginous effect of the curlicues and the grids and the panels of contrasting colours only occurred when one shifted one's eye from one element to another. This caused the patterns to reorganize themselves in perception, so that all of a sudden the yellow half-crescents, for instance, which a fraction of a second earlier had formed a part of the background, would be standing proud of the black hexagons, the purple cuneiforms, the red berries and the thousand other repeating elements. But unlike most patterns that are transformed by the roving eye, such as the beauty who turns into a hag and back into a beauty, due to its extreme complexity Churchwarden's hall had the peculiar quality of forcing the eye to rove further and further afield, making it impossible to rest one's gaze on any one element for more than the briefest moment. So as soon as the floor had resolved itself to perception, revealing one of its regularities as dominant and, as it were, the key to understanding the whole, another element would immediately push itself forward with the utmost importunity. Thus the eye would be drawn on, the psychological organization of the pattern would shift, and the very thing upon which one's feet were resting, which supported the whole of one's mass, skeletal and soft tissue alike, seemed to quake before one's eyes. The overall effect was to induce nausea. This was a purely psychological phenomenon, of course. But when one's mental world quakes, the world quakes with it. There's no two ways about it.

Eugenia was not frightened of these fractious symmetries, these vociferous motifs, these furiously argumentative hierarchies of colour. In fact she enjoyed their violent ambiguity. There are only seventeen types of two-dimensional symmetry, she told me, plus the infinite symmetry of the blank, none of which holds any dread for her. I was reminded of the old idea that there are only thirty-two different plots. I do not know what they are. It might be worth my while finding out, though. If I could work out which one I am in I might be able to do a better job of it.

When the mechanic arrived Eugenia left for the hotel, promising to take the room adjoining mine if it was available. I remained at the party a while longer, for politeness' sake, but my heart was no longer in it. The people skittering this way and that across Churchwarden's absurd entrance hall, the endless variations on the theme of human evasiveness, the novel yet familiar permutations of self-contempt, vanity, conceit, arrogance, humility and self-loathing, the endless, futile struggle to discover a meaning that can be imposed on life from the outside — the whole game had lost its interest for me.

Eugenia was back, and that was all that mattered.

Eugenia, to whose steady gaze the giddiest of patterns are a delight. Eugenia, for whom the meaning of life is always in question but never in doubt. Eugenia, who stands in the centre of her soul like a shaman ringed by her tribespeople, ready to hallucinate, to dream aloud, to be crushed by fear or raised up by yearning, all at a moment's notice.

(once upon a time there was a man called René Quite)

I walked home. The storm was still raging, the elements thrashing against their chains. What might those chains have been made of? Gravity, I suppose. Gravity, earth's only real attraction.

I wandered along the seafront watching the waves cracking their stubborn skulls against the massive sea wall. Sometimes black water erupted in dark fountains. Sometimes the waves were so huge they inundated the promenade, flooding the road with hungry wavelets that scurried this way and that in search of anything they could uproot and repossess for their master, the sea. I walked high on the grassy bank, out of the way of the water, where tightly ranked bathing huts faced the ocean's ferocity in orderly rows, the weaponless sentries of some mad, impoverished despot.

I was losing interest in the spectacle of the storm when a huge wave hit the sea wall unannounced, causing a dark, dull thud to reverberate through my feet. I stopped and turned. The wave was so large its onward rush was not stopped by the sly, concave wall. Instead it swept across the promenade and broke against the boulder-tusked bank at my feet. As the water swirled furiously only a few yards below me I saw, amid the dark confusion, a darker form announced. The sky was black, not a star in sight, and the mawkish sodium gloom of the streetlamps did not reach this far down the promenade. Straining to make out what I had glimpsed against the inky surface of the grimacing sea was more an effort of imagination than perception. At first I thought perhaps I was looking at the corpse of a dog or sheep. The water churned again as another wave scuttled up the back of the first. Then, as suddenly as if it had been ordained by a god, the water retreated. But something was left.

I clambered down the bank and jumped onto the promenade, which only a moment ago had been sub-merged under six feet of whirling water. At any moment the sea could have stretched out a fluid limb and taken me. But the shadowy presence in the darkness intrigued me, and I strode towards it. Then I froze. Before me, prone on the puddled concrete, limbs askew, was a child.

I could sense the sea preparing to advance again, eager to take its treasure back into its bosom, to caress it and play with it some more. So I grabbed the body under the arms and half-dragged, half-carried it towards the higher ground. Hoisting myself onto the low wall at the bottom of the boulder-studded bank I felt an obscure rumble pass

through the earth. Another huge wave had surged over the
sea wall and onto the promenade. Swiftly as in a dream, I
found myself engulfed. The water tugged at my trousers
and licked coldly at my skin. A moment later it gripped
me round the waist. I should have let the body go, cast it
back to placate the angry ocean, but I didn't even think of
it. Instead I clung on to a boulder with my knees,
crouching forwards as if in prayer. The body went light in
my arms. It was floating. I clung on as a wrecked mariner
clings to a spar or a fragment of mast. Slowly the wave
subsided, first sucking, then pulling, then dragging me
forcefully backwards with all its might. Feeling myself
begin to slide I scrabbled for something to grip on to with
my toes.

As suddenly as it had welled up the sea relinquished
its claim and fell back, sighing. I looked down. The child
was lying supine between my feet, lodged between the
toothed rocks. I had saved him: a boy of about ten or
twelve years old. He looked uncomfortable, his head
resting at an awkward angle between two sharp outcrops.
As gently as I could, I lifted him up and carried him onto
the grass.

His skin was pale and grey-green, just as a sea child's
ought to be. Laying him out I was at a loss what to do
next. Then I remembered: I should try to revive him.
Children, if kept in sufficiently cold water, can be pre-
served for astonishingly long periods of time. I angled
back his head, opened his mouth and kissed him full on
the lips. At first I thought I had forgotten to blow. But
no, I hadn't forgotten. I was blowing but his tongue was
in the way. I put my fingers in his mouth and pulled his

tongue forward. It was colder than any tongue I had ever touched. The effect was brutal. I kissed him again, this time managing to inflate his lungs. A wonderful feeling. Remembering the routine, I inflated his lungs a few more times, then beat down on his heart to force the blood around his body. Then I blew in more air. I continued this procedure for I don't know how long, inflating him, beating his heart, inflating him again, beating his heart again.

Gradually, or perhaps suddenly, I was overwhelmed by a sense of my own absurdity. Drenched in salt water, immured in darkness, invisible even to myself, kneeling yards from the furious ocean, I was inflating the lungs and massaging the heart of a corpse. The boy was cold as ice, had certainly been dead for hours, probably for days, and possibly for years. I ceased my anguished rebellion and lay down on the floor, panting. The two of us lay there together quietly side by side, me breathing, he not. I wondered if we looked alike.

Another vast wave crashed blindly into the wall, sending a shock wave through the air and the earth. High up on dry land though I was, I felt distinctly unsafe. The usual boundaries were not being observed. I wondered if the boy had perhaps come to fetch me, and if the sea would not now come for us both and carry us off. I wouldn't have minded. The boy didn't seem unhappy. It might have been fun, the two of us together, surfing and plummeting among the rollers, swimming with the fishes, sinking, dissolving.

I got up. The boy did not. I looked down at him. I couldn't leave him there, he was helpless on his own. He would have been better off in the sea. At least there he wouldn't stink. For a long time I wondered if should I throw him back.

In the end I decided I would take him to the hotel. I carried him draped over my shoulder like a long, thin sack of onions. He hung there, uncomplaining, his head dangling down over my chest, his feet tapping gently against the small of my back. We made a lugubrious couple. But it was late, it was stormy, and nobody was around to interrogate us. If they had I don't know what we would have told them. Certainly not the truth.

When the boy and I arrived back in my room I dried him off, picked the seaweed from his pockets, and gave his hair a rub with a warm towel. He was an attractive youth, open and full of curiosity, with big plans for the future. I wrapped him in a sheet and put him to sleep in the bath. He's in the deep-freeze now, one of those cabinet models. It's like a great big toy box. He's sitting up, surrounded by lambs and Christmas turkeys. I'll leave him there until somebody comes to claim him.

Eugenia has apologized for running away. She says she realized when she was halfway home that she didn't at all mind what she had seen me doing, but that it took her a long time to believe that she didn't mind, so strong is the presumption that one should feel humiliated and angry in such a situation.

Our relationship has entered a new period of openness. Eugenia has stopped painting so many landscapes and is concentrating her attention on figure work. She paints me most of the time, herself the rest of the time. Sitting as a model for her is hard work because she has become very interested in sexuality and insists that I should be sexually aroused while she paints me. So I sit there dreaming of anything that might help keep my prick pumped up, masturbating if necessary, as Eugenia paints. It is all very harmless. Sometimes Eugenia photographs me, trying to catch the moment when I lose myself in the rictus of orgasm and my cock spits out its dollops of white blindness. She paints herself from photographs which I take of her, sometimes with her long capable fingers pushed inside her vulva or pressing her clitoris as she writhes, bites her lip, seethes and shudders in orgasm. Sometimes we take pictures of the two of us interpenetrating. It is all eminently harmless. Sometimes we go to prostitutes and Eugenia sketches as I fuck, or I photograph as Eugenia fucks. We cover all the angles, all the possibilities. There is no harm in any of them.

Her paintings are very red, very fleshy. She paints our genitals like vicious blooms on strange desert plants, weird pink succulents. Our faces she draws on afterwards, impassive observers of our own most intimate frenzy, ideally suspended between desire and repulsion.

Eugenia thinks I should go back to university and teach. She says we need the money. She has explained to the faculty what happened to me, and my job is being kept open. I tell her I wouldn't know what to teach, I don't know anything of the subjects I used to talk about. She sympathizes, and secretly approves.

I now have memories of the time before. They do not run together, they do not form a line, or even a pattern, but still, they are there. If I could run a thread through them then I could perhaps fight behind the banner of my own name.

Brian Smith has not yet returned. But he sent me a brief fax saying that all the evidence pointed to the fact that I was spatially and temporally continuous with René Quite. Says I made a proper twat of myself in a library, climbing up a shelving unit to retrieve a book and pulling the entire caboodle down on my head in the process. One bystander claims I cried out 'Schopenhauer' as I fell. The rest, he says, is the pathetic fantasy of an overwrought, mid-ranking academic brain. It doesn't matter to me either way. I have to be someone, after all. René Quite is only a name, albeit a rather odd-sounding one.

Soon it will be my birthday. Eugenia has organized a party for me. That is to say, she has asked the proprietor to organize one. She is going to invite all the people I have met since I lost my memory. This will encourage me to put my recent experiences into some kind of narrative order, giving me a starting point from which to arrange the memories from before. If I can create a demand for it, a past will emerge. That is Eugenia's idea.

I feel trepidation, for the understanding is that I will make some kind of public summary of my last couple of months. I do not know if this is possible, or even desirable. I feel trepidation, for I will be the unstated purpose of this gathering, the hollow centre. I, the hero who cowers before the empty citadel of himself, eyeing the gates with dread in case they should be opened, and he be permitted to enter.

I must learn to navigate by the fixed points of these

acquaintances. Having found my bearings, I must then set sail into the past, and circumnavigate my evasions. When I arrive I will collect specimens and draw myself a chart. But I do not think there is anything there. I do not think there ever was.

Eugenia says there is nothing on the surface of the moon either, but that doesn't mean it isn't worth visiting to take in the view. But I have always had a good view. I have seen it all, in my way. What I long for now are dense thickets, labyrinthine caves, and deep wells. I crave the intimacy of dark scents, the fragility of the particular, and the bafflement of strong emotion. My theoretical days are over.

Once upon a time there was a man called René Quite.

(the corpse of time)

At the Grand Hotel, Scarby, a dinner was held in honour of the birthday of Mr René Quite (DPhil), recently recovered from a bout of childish stupidity. Also present at the dinner were Mrs Eugenia Quite, Dr Nous (BM, MRCPsch), Mr Barclay (BPess), Nurse Sue (DipNurse), Mr Effie Rance (Proprietor, the Grand Hotel), Mr Eric Churchwarden (CDL) and Mr Brian Smith (DipSM).

After the coffee and liqueurs were served Mrs Eugenia Quite proposed that the guests should take it in turns to tell each other stories. She invited her husband to start them off. Mr René Quite rose slowly to his feet.

Speaking hesitantly and looking downwards often, he spoke in low and somewhat confused tones.

'I have no story. I know no stories. I have heard other people's stories, but never, ever have I had a story of my own. Stories are processions in time. Failure flanks the route, and the awaiting dignity is Death. Stories takes courage.

'For many years I had theories. Theories, which deck the world in a suit of perfect stillness, visible only to the elect. Theories: the corpse of time, butchered and bottled in truth. Perhaps once upon a time I could have entertained you with one of those theories, dressed it up as a story and wheeled it out in narrative form. Maybe some people would have been satisfied by this. But now I am no longer possessed even of theories. I have memories, but they exist in a heap, as though they had been delivered to my door by lorry, paid for by the ton.

'I am better than I was. I have relinquished my ambition to dominate reality with ideas. I have laid down my weapons. But still I have no stories.

'Once upon a time there was a man who knew no stories. That man was me. That man is me.'

Mr Quite was about to resume his seat when it occurred to him that he should show his friends that he had not lost hope. 'Wish me luck,' he said with a smile. The request was answered with smiles and raised glasses. René Quite resumed his seat. Resting her hand on his, Eugenia Quite consoled her husband.

Mr Effie Rance, after first looking this way and that to see whether anyone else was inclined to take the floor, rose slowly and decorously to his feet. After first wishing Mr Quite the best of luck in his search for a story, he began. His ponderous Yorkshire vowels and flashes of self-depreciating wit kept the gathering riveted throughout his tale, which the reader should be warned contains passages of a bawdy nature.

(point blank)

'The story I am going to share with you concerns the subject popularly known as *filth*,' he began, looking about the table with generous eyes, 'equally popularly as *love*, and otherwise referred to by a combination of these two concepts bound together in some word or phrase chosen for its ability to express the precise proportion of damnation, exaltation, disgust, reverence, gravity and humour felt by the particular speaker for the dark act of coupling ... and sometimes tripling, ahem.

'As a young man I found myself troubled, or perhaps blessed (who knows?), with a mildly perverse fantasy. In this fantasy I saw myself shooting my muck directly onto a beautiful girl's face. The sight of her soft skin, her delicate nose, her cheekbones, her lips, her lashes, her proud neck, beslubbered all over with my very own semen, so excited me that my cock just kept pumping and pumping. It was grand. I had seen as much done in illicit films, but had never had the opportunity to try it for myself. To be honest, I was unsure whether this fantasy was acceptable or not. In my book, the perversion of the sexual instinct from the simple act of procreation is a very good thing indeed. If it didn't happen spontaneously it would be necessary to introduce it as part of our sexual education.

'But the intentional humiliation of another person is a very different matter. Half of me, or perhaps three-quarters, believed my fantasy to be nothing more pernicious than a reverent desire to see my sticky seed, bodily token of my solemn adoration, anointing a beautiful woman's face (for me always the most delightful part of a woman's body, transcending even the buttocks for loveliness). But one has to be careful about these things, and a part of me suspected that in truth I was indulging the base urge to humiliate, to objectify some innocent woman and reduce her to the status of toilet paper. Older now, and I hope a little wiser, I wonder how I could ever have thought of semen as being on a par with excrement. How could one half of the equation that produces human life ever be considered some mere dregs?'

At this point the mellifluous Irishman Mr Barclay broke in, quipping gloomily that he'd never heard spunk better described.

Mr Rance took a dialectical approach to this barracking. 'Then you consider the sexual act to be part of a process of purification?'

'I do. And it explains a lot,' said Mr Barclay, turning to address the company in earnest. 'The first man, the first woman, they were pure. Everyone knows that. Adman and Ivy they were called. They lived in the Garden of Stink. They had fun. Difficult to believe it now, I know, but they did. But in order to maintain their astonishing level of perfection it was necessary for them to constantly process and expel their imperfections. One day, accidentally, or perhaps out of curiosity, they mixed their imperfections together. Soon after that their first child was born. The race has been degenerating ever since. The degeneration is systematic, consisting of a fifty per cent drop in quality with every new generation. It can be demonstrated algebraically. One seven is seven, two sevens are both seven, three sevens are all of them seven, and so it goes on till the maws of hell swallow us up...'

Mr Barclay was becoming heated. His face had reddened, and his head was twisting and turning stubbornly on his neck in a manner reminiscent of a distressed stallion. Mr Rance was still on his feet, patiently waiting to be allowed to finish his own tale. Mrs Eugenia Quite, self-elected symposiarch, stepped in, asking the errant symposiast with utmost delicacy, if he would please shut his gob till it was his turn to speak, as she for one was keen to hear the end of Mr Rance's dirty story. Gracelessly, Mr Barclay complied.

Mr Rance continued. 'A bitter tale, Mr Barclay, and a false one, both in fact and in spirit. But I'm sure we'll have time to argue the point later. So, to continue with my story, suffice to say that my youthful shame and self-doubt was such that this fantasy was not one I would have suggested to a woman of my own accord. Rather, I hoped that some day I might be asked. Somewhat optimistic of me, you might have thought. But one day, to my surprise, a girl I was involved with did just that. She was a sensitive girl, and very beautiful, and I had been itching to try this manoeuvre with her for some time. It seems that her understanding of her fellow man, which was never less than piercing, had somehow led her to an awareness of my feelings. Or perhaps I had been talking in my sleep. Either way, on one occasion, when our sex play was well advanced, sensing I was ready to ejaculate, she issued the much longed-for invitation. "If you want to you can come on my face," she said, with a lovely open smile and not a hint of embarrassment or shame. I was charmed and delighted. "I'd love to," I replied. "I'd utterly love to."

'My only problem was that the girl was standing up at the time. And when I asked her to lie down she refused point blank, on the grounds that it wouldn't feel comfortable that way. Even so, she said, she'd like to see me ejaculate on her face. I pointed out to her that even at the age of sixteen, when my sexual fervour was at its theoretical peak, the feat she envisaged would not have been an easy one. But for a heavy drinker in his late twenties, the thing was impossible. Once again she repeated that she would very much like to see me come on her face, if I was up to the job. I could sense she was digging in her heels.

'So I fetched a chair from the dining room, masturbating all the while to keep up my strength. Placing the chair in front of her, I mounted it. Still the distance appeared too great for me to bridge. Still she was insistent that I should satisfy my fantasy. So I fetched a second chair and balanced it as best I could atop the first. I was a few tyres lighter in those days, but even so my gymnastic abilities were sorely tested as I clambered onto my makeshift scaffold and hesitantly assumed an upright position. At last the geometry seemed propitious. There she was, her pretty little face only inches from the tip of my knob, smiling excitedly, apparently eager to be doused in hot cum.

'But fresh difficulties emerged. For every time I gave my cock a tug the chairs wobbled from side to side. It was like trying to wank while crossing a rope bridge. Nonetheless, I persisted. In spite of all, I persisted. And after a time I did indeed succeed in falling into some kind of rhythm. As with so many other things in life, as I'm sure everyone gathered round the table this evening is well aware, success in love is very much a matter of finding the correct rhythm. And so I entered a period of hope. But soon I sensed that something was terribly wrong. Excited though I was, the clock was ticking, and not a drop of ejaculate forthcoming.'

Mr Rance, hot with emotion, paused to take a drink.

'I continued, oh, of course I continued. But it seemed my font was dry. My girlfriend gradually started to look bored. Inevitably, morale suffered. And in the end, after all our struggles together, try as I might to inspire him, my little soldier lay down and died.'

Here Rance came to a full stop. He seemed to be contemplating the image he had just described. As at a state funeral, after the cannons have sounded but before the bugle's lament is heard, the gathering held its silence. Then, with a wistful sigh, he continued.

'It seems that the supple, swaying posture I was forced to adopt in order to prevent my tower from collapsing had caused me to relax the muscles of the inner thigh. I didn't know it at the time, but it seems I had unintentionally stumbled upon the Tantric Buddhist technique for inhibiting ejaculation. I read about it in a phone-box in Hampstead, many years later. It was on some sort of special offer...'

His words trailed away. A silence ensued which Mr René Quite found difficult to bear, as his good friend and one time shagging companion Mr Effie Rance remained standing, his big, bald, pudgy head hanging down like an oversized fruit.

'She humiliated you!' Mr Quite cried in sympathy.

'She did,' Mr Rance concurred, raising his head to fill once more the gap left by his fallen gaze. 'And a rare thing it is too. For normally no one is quick enough, I get there so promptly myself.'

The company smiled. Mrs Eugenia Quite stood and kissed Mr Rance gallantly on the cheek, to thank him for his engaging yarn, and because she was now ready to take the floor herself.

(well and truly interred)

'My story too is sad, I'm afraid. It's about a friend of mine, a woman who made her living as a sculptor. It's the story of her tombstone. She made it herself, and liked it so much, she died especially for it.'

'Here, here,' rumbled Mr Barclay, unable to allow a reference to death pass by without expressing his approval.

'Thank you, Mr Barclay. But for me her death is not a cause for celebration. She was a dear friend and I miss her painfully. Her name was Jessica.

'Jessica fell in love with a piece of yellow Italian marble. *Marmaros*, the shining stone, created from the compacted and fossilized bones of billions upon billions of ancient sea creatures, death piled up by the ton, converted into limestone by massive pressure, then crystallized by heat. It was a large block, only slightly too small for a life-size horse and rider. Jessica wasn't doing very well at the time, and was certainly not in a position to invest time and money in a major piece without the security of a commission to guarantee payment, but she liked this great hunk of rock so much that she scraped the money together anyway and had it shipped back to England. When it arrived she immediately discovered that it almost filled her studio. All her other work had to be put to one side to make room for this vast block.

'She ceased work on all her other projects and lived with the marble for three months, spending her days taking its measure with her eyes and hands, sometimes pressing her whole body against it, even sniffing it. She told me it was the most beautiful piece of rock she had ever seen. It had emerged from the quarry as an almost perfect hexahedron, the obtuse angles of five of its six faces undulating like the muscles on the haunches of a bull. The sixth face was bitten and crenellated, and scored from top right to bottom left with a deep fissure. Jessica didn't know how deep the fissure would run. It was possible that it would flaw the whole block. But she felt instinctively that it was superficial, and thought herself sufficiently attuned to the rock to trust this feeling.

'In one face of the block she could see a child, in one the ocean, in one a forest. In the fissure she saw death, which appears to run deep, rending everything from itself, but is really a superficial thing, more a furrow in which life takes seed than a gash through which it bleeds. That's how Jessica saw it, anyway. The uppermost face, which she could only view by leaning over the top of a tall stepladder and pressing her cheek to her studio ceiling, seemed to her a broad expanse of land, with hillocks, wide valleys, plateaux and slopes. She could see the foundations of fallen houses and tumbledown sheepfolds. She could see a dried-up lake bed where abundant crops grew.

'But these were only the surfaces. Jessica was a sculptor and her real interest was in the forms the rock still contained, the solid truth shrouded by the rough hewn ideal the quarry men had imposed. She found it hard to put a chisel to the rock but, after having spent over a hundred days contemplating it, she felt as ready as she ever would be.

'She started with the fissure. She needed to know how deep it ran, so she selected a heavy chisel. After a few sharp taps a great flake of marble, a picture-window-sized scallop of opaque yellow stone, peeled away and shattered against the concrete floor, leaving behind it a smooth, shallow hollow. Now the marble was ready.

'The next day Jessica woke up knowing what she wanted to make. It was to be a woman — a fertile, man-fucking, cock-sucking, baby-making, culture-shaping woman, with hips like a cradle, powerful hands, slim limbs, tidy breasts, full lips parted as if in greeting, her hair tied up to show off her elegant neck, eyes smiling, brow calm, head erect, and her weight on the front foot as she moved forward in pursuit of her desire. Jessica didn't need a model. She knew the woman already existed, fully formed, inside the marble. So she set about uncovering her.

'She worked day and night for two months. She thought of nothing else. She hardly ate, and she saw nobody.

'When the figure was finally almost ready, only wanting polishing to be complete, Jessica invited me round to see it. She phoned me on Sunday and we agreed I would visit the following Tuesday. When I arrived at her studio I went straight in. What I saw horrified me. The woman was destroyed. That is to say, part of her remained, but her beautiful head was on the floor amongst the shards of marble, and just to one side lay one of her lithe arms. I asked Jessica what had happened. She told me that the woman had been too large, or too small, she wasn't sure which, but either way she wasn't satisfied with her. She had been satisfied with her at first, very satisfied. For a while, indeed, she had thought the piece the best she had ever done. But when looking at the shards she had realized that something was wrong, there was too much waste, or too little, she couldn't tell which. Since restoring the block to its original state was not possible, her only option was to rework what remained.

'As Jessica was explaining this, her assistant – a delicate man with wiry arms and wispy hair who normally never spoke unless he had to – blurted out that it was madness. Then he left the room in shame and annoyance. But Jessica didn't seem mad, she seemed very lucid – unusually so, in fact. We had lunch, I wished her luck, and left her to her work.

'Two months later Jessica invited me back to see the result, which her assistant had just started to polish that day. A vague sense of foreboding made me insist that she should make time to see me the very next morning. Even so, I arrived too late. A ravishingly powerful female figure, full of elegance and desire, identical so far as I could see to the last, unless it was perhaps a little more perfect, a little more alive, a little more balanced and organic in its volumes, was standing there before me, already half dismantled.

'Jessica's assistant was ashen-faced. Sick with anger and disappointment, he moved around the studio like he was haunting the place. But Jessica herself was serene. Ignoring my expressions of shock and dismay she directed my attention to the shards that lay around the base of the sculpture. These were now of three types. The first type related to the emergence of the first form from the block, the second related to the emergence of the second form from the first form, and the third was produced by the first stages of the current work. The second and third type of fragment were especially beautiful: here a nose, there an ear, and here again a whole hand, all with raw cut rock on the reverse. Inner and outer, formed and formless, were related in what Jessica described playfully as her growing heap of insights.

'A year and a day since Jessica had taken delivery of the great marble block she was finishing work on her fifth figure. I had seen them all. Each was identical to the last in all but size, yet each somehow contrived to surpass the last in the indefinable subtleties of space, motion and rhythm. Each time Jessica completed a figure, her assistant pleaded with her to stop. But each time she pressed ahead, unable to resist the temptation to add to the growing heap of rubble that lay around the work itself, and now stood as high as a mountain cairn.

'The most recent figure was no more than thirty inches high, which made it smaller than some of the larger pieces of rocky detritus. At this point Jessica stopped. She was satisfied: the work was ready. Taking the fifth figure from the plinth that had supported it while she worked, Jessica lay it down on the cairn of rubble as if upon a funeral bier or rocky pyre. Then we went out and had a big lunch together. Jessica regained the appetites for food and conversation and company that for over a year had been subsumed by her desire to realize her intentions in stone. I had never known her happier, brighter, more full of life, more attuned to things, more at one with herself than she was that day.

'The rest of the story I only know from her assistant, for I never saw Jessica alive again. Her last words as we left the restaurant were that she wanted to be with her work. It seems that while we were out at lunch some workmen came, on Jessica's orders, and cleared the pile of glorious rubble away. They cleared it up and took it to a processing plant, where it underwent the procedure known as reconstitution. Shortly after Jessica left me she killed herself, driving her car headlong into a rocky cutting, whose sheer walls of powdery red sandstone I had often heard her admire. In her pocket she was carrying the instructions for her burial. The cairn of shards, together with the statue itself, had already been reformed as a highly polished, regular hexahedron of precise dimensions, a perfected version of the form in which the block had emerged from the quarry. It was delivered directly to a graveyard near Jessica's studio, and it was waiting there when her body was brought from the mortuary.

'There is no inscription on that vast rock, which towers above the other ornaments in the graveyard. Rather than standing at the head of Jessica's grave, it lies directly over it, as if ensuring by its mass that she remains well and truly interred. But in its highly polished surfaces it is possible, in the right light, to detect fragments of the five women, fragments which survived the process of reconstitution. Here an eye, there a nipple, here again a lock of hair, these morsels of the beauty Jessica discovered, rediscovered, then discovered all over again, could, if you didn't know the truth, be mistaken for scraps of fossils, the lithic memory of the ancient creatures of the sea.

'That is my story.'

Once again the party was moved to silence. This time the mood was sorrowful, as each person wondered at the immense strength of character and strange inspiration of the woman whose awesome end had just been described to them. Mrs Eugenia Quite called for the glasses to be refreshed, then proposed a toast to her dead friend Jessica, which was agreed to with enthusiasm.

Next to speak was the distinguished psychiatrist, Dr Nous.

(don't be a fool)

'My story is a happy story,' began Dr Nous.

'Then it's fiction you'll be telling us?' asked Mr Barclay pointedly.

'No, it is the truth,' answered Dr Nous, smiling indulgently at Mr Barclay's pessimism.

'Someone fetch a psychiatrist,' whispered Mr Barclay, turning to face the company. 'The man's stream of consciousness has burst its banks. You go to the phone while I sit here smiling inanely at him.'

Everybody laughed, except Dr Nous, who addressed the heckler with his customary gravity.

'It is a happy story, yes, though not one I hope which altogether avoids life's tragic aspect. Let us say it has a happy ending.'

'Why is it always the ending that is happy,' Mr Barclay sang out despondently, 'and never the middle? I live in the middle. I always have done. The thing's a swizz. They're tricks, these cheery yarns of yours, springes to catch woodcocks. It is the murky middle that we inhabit, not the happy ending.'

'Not so, Mr Barclay,' responded Nous, modulating his voice as if addressing a bright but confused child. 'It is the possibility of a happy ending that motivates the middle, that drains off its stagnant waters, and determines the shape of the story as a whole. This is the case even in a tragedy, over which the possibility of a happy ending hovers like a topsy-turvy curse, even though we know it will not happen. The truth is that without the possibility of a happy ending there would be no movement and no risk. Death in such cases is immediate, though the hair and nails might continue to grow, perhaps for several decades.'

'Go on with you, Dr Nous. Raise me from the dead first and explain how you did it afterwards.'

At this point Eugenia Quite lost her patience with Mr Barclay and told him that he was to keep his big poisonous trap shut until it was his turn to speak, when he could hypnotize the company with his tales of death, failure and decay for all he was worth. Mr Barclay complied, this time making apology for his vociferation, which he explained was for him a chronic condition that Mrs Quite could, if she wished to be charitable, regard as a biological matter.

'An interesting point, Mr Barclay,' broke in Dr Nous, 'and not altogether unrelated to the theme of the case I am about to describe to you. It is a simple case, and yet one of the most satisfying I have dealt with.

'It concerns a young boy, seven years of age. When I first saw him he had just about wasted away. The physicians had done all the tests they could think of. They had investigated his body from every point of view, and they could find nothing whatsoever wrong with him. But something was wrong with him, because he couldn't walk, he slept hardly at all, he ate little, said nothing, and refused even to write or draw. Yet it was clear that his senses were unimpaired, that his intellect was lively, that he enjoyed company and appreciated any attention that was shown to him.

'When other children on the ward played, he watched them eagerly, though not without a hint of something like disdain. The nurses would sit with him and tell him stories, to try to keep him cheerful. Sometimes he would laugh out loud at a joke, but he would quickly stifle his laughter, covering his mouth with his hand, even pushing his whole fist into his mouth if necessary. He greeted his mother with friendly eyes, but little more. His father he honoured with a complete cessation of communication, bringing himself as close to catatonia as conscious determination imaginably could. Yet when his father left, after having spent an hour by the boy's bed, which he did religiously three times a week, the boy would smile a great smile of satisfaction and pleasure.

'As far as the boy himself was concerned this was all there was to observe, because although he was known to have been an exceptionally articulate child up until a few months ago, he could not be persuaded to answer questions of any sort.

'The parents themselves had no idea what had happened. The father regretted having spoken harshly to him the last time he had seen him prior to the onset of his illness. He couldn't remember the context, or exactly what was said, but he remembered the boy prattling on nonsensically, as children do, and he remembered telling him off for it. He didn't think he had been particularly severe. The father had set off the next day on a long business trip and hadn't seen the child again for a whole month, during which time a gradual deterioration occurred. The mother described how the boy had shed layers of activity, growing ever more serious and taciturn. When the boy refused to get out of bed, collapsing on the floor in a heap when his mother tried to make him stand up, she finally called a doctor. The boy was admitted to hospital and the father flew back to be with him.

'An unusual case. One could easily have written it off as malingering, or attention-seeking, except that the boy had previously seemed very happy, and when he became ill he expressed no pain, made no claim on people's pity, and demanded no special favour. If anything, he seemed to be eschewing attention. I tried everything I could to persuade him to communicate. I played with toys in front of him, I played with a computer, I showed him paintings, I played music, I gave him paper and crayons, I gave him clay. Still he made no response. Then one day, after I had been encouraging him to draw, to no effect, I turned to speak to a nurse who had a question about the boy's treatment. As we were talking something startled us. A paper aeroplane had swished by and crashed on the other side of the ward. I turned and looked at the boy. He was impassive. But there was no doubt that the dart had come from his direction. Quelling my excitement, I casually offered him more paper and started making a dart myself. He didn't respond. He appeared to be angry with himself.

'Next day I showed him pictures of aeroplanes, of birds in flight, of hang-gliders. I showed him videos of rockets taking off, of bats careering through the dusk, of flying fish surging out of the sea. Every creature that flaps, glides or plummets through the ocean of air that envelops the earth, every man-made device for defying earth's gravity, I showed to him. Try as he might, wilful though he was, he could neither hide nor extinguish every trace of his enthusiasm.

'And so I rang a friend who has a private pilot's licence, and arranged for him to take the boy up the very next day.

'It was an icy winter's morning, the air clear and bright as diamond. I carried the boy into the plane and strapped him into his seat. He showed scant sign of excitement. If anything he seemed to have deteriorated a little during the night. He slumped like an unstuffed doll, his wan face grey and waxy as a cadaver's. In his eyes, however, I could detect traces of a new anxiety. I tried to engage him in conversation, but he only stared at the window. As the pilot went through his final checks, the boy's interest, such as it was, seemed only to wane. But when the pilot switched on the engine, the sound seemed to sear through the boy, and he began to sweat and shake in his seat. I was scared for him, and felt tempted to put a stop to the experiment there and then. But I reminded myself that there was nothing physically wrong with the child, and that people are seldom killed by their emotions, unless their bodies are already failing. A few minutes later we took off. As we did so the boy let out a gasp, then relaxed.

'Very soon he was sitting erect in his seat, his face pressed against the window. Gradually, as we swooped and turned across open country, sometimes dipping low over fields and hedges, sometimes soaring to the very limit of the plane's climbing ability, the little boy came back to life. When I judged the time was right, I asked him if he was having fun. He nodded. I suggested he told the pilot where he wanted us to fly. Without thinking twice he asked the pilot to go as high as he could. The pilot did so, and explained to the boy how the controls worked.

'Eventually, when fuel was low and it was time to return to the airfield, I asked the boy very casually what his father had said to him before he had gone away on his business trip. The boy thought for a minute, not about his answer, which was already on his lips straining to get out, but about whether or not he should, or could, tell me. Finally he decided that he could. He spoke four words to me. At first he said them so quietly they were completely drowned out by the roar of the engine. I asked him to repeat himself. He paused for a moment, then sharp as a siren he hollered out, "Don't be a fool." That, and nothing more.

'It seems that the father, in his desire to stop the child's burbling, which I suppose must have been irritating him, had said these words to him. The boy, who didn't understand what he had done wrong, was an earnest learner and very keen to please. And so he had asked the father what a fool was. "Someone who makes a spectacle of themselves in order to win approval," the father had told him. It seems that the boy, an exceptionally intelligent and serious-minded child, had thought this definition through carefully, and applied his father's injunction diligently. As he discovered more and more of his behaviour that fell or could easily be brought within the meaning of the term, he weaned himself off it. And so he ended up in silence, barely moving, doing nothing beyond fulfilling his basic physical functions, and even that without much relish.'

The pensive silence that followed Dr Nous's story was finally broken by Mr Effie Rance, who was bouncing up and down in his chair with excitement and glee.

'That boy was me!' he shouted. 'That boy was me. I was that boy. What a story, what a story. It's the story of my life, of my early life. Of course, I never had such determination. I never had such style, such acuity. But nevertheless, in a small way, I have lived that story. I thank you, Dr Nous. You have touched me.'

'And I will touch you too,' declared Nurse Sue, springing to her feet as though inspired, her eyes flashing with playful malevolence, heightened with just a hint of stage fright. 'Touch you, and appal you too, with the story of a friend of mine, an old lover in fact. His name is Aloysius, and he's a doctor. And when he was at university a funny thing happened to him. Funny peculiar, not funny ha-ha, because it very nearly resulted in his death, or if not his death then ... I don't know what.' Her face was flushed from the wine she had drunk, but she was alert and filled with desire to outdo the storytellers who had preceded her. She paused to take a sip of water, then once more addressed the table in her fine, bold voice.

(the oracular seriousness
of the storyteller)

'Arriving late for his second year at college, having been unavoidably delayed by civil war on the obscure Pacific island where he had spent the summer alone, adventuring in the wilderness, Aloysius found that the friends he had hoped to share a house with had already made their arrangements without him. This wasn't because he was unpopular. On the contrary, he was a charming, exceptionally attractive young man, good at sports, and naturally kind and thoughtful, to men and women alike. And good in bed too.' Sue hesitated, seemingly distracted by a memory, and her expression changed from the oracular seriousness of the storyteller to something altogether more personal. Holding up her two hands some eight or ten inches apart as if measuring a fish, she grinned broadly and said without lewdness, 'His willy's this long, and he knows very well how to use it for the best. And as I'm sure Eugenia will agree, any woman who says that size doesn't count is a liar or a virgin. But I digress.'

'Swept away by fond memories,' cried out Mr Rance jovially, raising his glass to drink Nurse Sue's health, clasping her bright eyes in his as he imbibed. It seemed these two kindly sensualists were becoming friends.

The other guests looked questioningly at Eugenia. She turned from face to face, a modest half-smile illuminating her already beautiful features. 'It's true. I'm sorry, but it is.' She laughed. Many shades of disappointment and delight could be discriminated on the faces of the men present.

'As I was saying,' Nurse Sue continued, 'he was popular with both sexes, and it wasn't that his friends didn't want to live with him, it was simply that they thought he was dead. Everyone did, his family included. The reason for this presumption is a story in itself. Aloysius had gone to this Pacific island in order to climb in the mountains. He had gone alone, without the benefit of maps, into the jungle homeland of warlike tribes, some of them with a tradition of cannibalism, in a country with a history of political instability, at a time when armed insurrection was being widely predicted.

'He went there with his eyes open. He was very capable of looking after himself, being a strong athlete and trained in martial arts, but even so, when war broke out and heavy fighting was reported in the very area he had set out to explore, and Aloysius failed to return as expected, the people who cared about him held out little hope. They were wrong, because in the end he came back safe and sound, if a little emaciated. Exactly what happened to Aloysius out there in the jungle would take too long to relate. Suffice to say he had emerged from a terrifying ordeal more or less unscathed, having had what he described as, cuisine apart, a thoroughly stimulating time.

'This little holiday was typical of Aloysius during this period of his life. He was one of the most reckless people I've ever met. He used to say that if an activity didn't carry a five per cent chance of death or serious injury, it wasn't worth getting out of bed for. He wasn't fond of brute risk-taking, though. He scorned the idea of Russian roulette, which he thought altogether too easy and unskilled a game. But he relished any activity in which his intelligence and strength and determination could be pitted against fate. His family called it a death wish, but I personally don't think there was anything remotely suicidal about him.

'You see, Aloysius considered danger a forgotten bio-logical necessity. Everyone considers it necessary to piss and shit and eat, he used to say, and most sensible people these days consider fucking to be an appetite which, while needing no encouragement, requires no suppression either. Ambition is highly approved of, and the desire for social status is widely esteemed. The only natural appetite that has yet to be redeemed from the sin bin is the appetite for risk. We squander this urge, Aloysius believed, in tedious and socially harmful activities like driving too fast and drinking, smoking and eating too much. Aloysius was almost evangelical about this. He believed that a prolonged near-death experience, in which the individual is forced to use all their physical and mental resources to avert the catastrophe of personal destruction, is one of the greatest luxuries this world has to offer. And as with sex, he used to say, it needn't cost money in order to be great.

'I hope I've given you some idea of what sort of person my friend Aloysius was back then. If I've gone on a bit, it's only because I think his view on this subject was unusual, and possibly has some relevance to the story I'm going to tell you. What that relevance might be, I'm not at all sure, but there you go.

'So, arriving back at university, unable to afford the rent on a flat of his own, but unwilling to go back to the hysterical conviviality of a hall of residence overrun by insecure first year students, he decided instead to take lodgings. This had the advantage of being cheap, gave him the option of having meals prepared for him, and would free him from the more intrusive demands of what he considered to be the somewhat herd-like social life of the university.

'Because, you see, in some ways Aloysius was too popular for his own good. He had about him a certain sensuality and warmth, combined with an eager vulner-ability and a natural cheerfulness, that attracted many people to him whose feelings he did not reciprocate. Being almost painfully kind-hearted and never willing to hurt people who meant him no harm, he lived his life in perpetual fear of squandering time on people who bored him. And so, rather than risk joining a house of students whom he did not know, he decided instead to try living with a local family, who would of course be happy to leave him to his own devices.

'After checking out the options, he chose to move in with a family called the Ferns. They lived in a pleasant, rambling house close to the university. And, having a teenage son and daughter of their own, Aloysius imagined they would have little interest in his own affairs. On top of which, the rent they were asking was minuscule. The family seemed to be renting the room out more through a desire to see their large, and largely uninhabited, house put to some good use than for the extra money it might bring in. And they certainly didn't appear to want his company. They seemed an uncommonly happy family, very much absorbed in their own affairs, and spending as much time together as they could. When he went to look at the room, which was large and secluded and had its own bathroom, they didn't even ask him what subject he studied.

'And so he moved in. For the first few weeks he was out most of the time, catching up with the work he had missed, as well as catching up with his friends. In consequence he saw almost nothing of the family, leaving the house to run around the park long before they got up in the mornings, and arriving back in the evening long after they had gone to bed. The family lived in close proximity to one another, their snug living and sleeping accommodation tucked away in one small corner of the commodious building, and so even when the family and Aloysius were in the house at the same time their paths seldom crossed.

'But as his schedule settled down and he was able to stay in bed a little longer in the mornings, he started sharing breakfast with the family, and in that way he got to know them. Breakfast was the biggest meal of the Ferns' day. They're the only people I've ever heard of who took the dieticians' advice seriously and ate their main meal in the morning. The whole family breakfasted together, and though the father read the paper as he ate, and the children often did homework, and the mother cooked, there was still plenty of conversation around the table.

'They seemed an exceptionally close family, with aston-ishingly little friction between them. The sixteen-year-old son got on cosily with his pretty seventeen-year-old sister. The parents were scrupulous in favouring each of the children equally, so that if one parent was showing special attention to one child, the other parent would make a point of showing affection to their sibling. The mother and father were loving and respectful towards one another, clearly still attracted to each other after twenty years of marriage. The father worked hard, often spending more than twelve hours a day at his office. But what free time he had, he devoted to his family, and when jobs around the house needed doing, the children would always help.

'As far as Aloysius could tell, the daughter had com-plete freedom to come and go as she pleased. The parents never batted an eyelid if she suggested she might want to stay overnight at a friend's house, though for one reason or another she would never end up doing so, always finding some excuse to come home instead. The parents were happy to ferry her wherever she wanted to go, and to pick her up again afterwards, or else to give her money for taxis if she preferred. In return for their generosity, the demands the daughter made on her parents' time were very reasonable.

'Likewise with pocket money, the parents stressed that there was plenty of money to go around, and that the children should set their own limits on spending. The children responded by spending only modest amounts, considering all their purchases carefully, and only buying things that would be of real value to them.

'After a while, so extraordinarily harmonious and comfortable was the family life of the Ferns, Aloysius started to suspect that they must belong to some kind of cult, and that the almost incredibly sensible, contented behaviour of the children was achieved through fear, or brainwashing, or religious coercion. He started listening carefully to the breakfast-time conversation for any hints of what might be underpinning this abnormal complaisance. He heard nothing suspicious. Intrigued and somewhat incredulous, he began keeping tabs on the family's movements, trying to work out if there were any occasions when the whole family regularly left the house and returned together.

'He soon discovered that they went out every Saturday morning for about three hours. These appointments were never spoken of at breakfast. Aloysius decided that if there was any organized weirdness going on, that was when it took place. So he persuaded a friend to tail them. It turned out that they were attending ice-skating lessons together.

'In the end, after listening and watching them closely for several weeks, Aloysius carefully concluded that the only cult they belonged to was that most respectable of our cultural institutions, the nuclear family. In conversation parents and children alike referred to "the Family" and "the Ferns" with abnormal frequency. They made jokes about themselves, as well as frequent appreciative references to their solidarity and team spirit. Other branches of the family were mocked and subtly criticized. Outsiders were regarded as just that, and though they were shown respect (the Ferns being great believers in the value of hospitality), they were never fully admitted into the family group.

'After a while Aloysius began to feel that the Ferns lived all together in one cosy corner of their great Victorian house because the extra space around them, and their large garden outside, were necessary to insulate them from the wider world. Their favourite activity was watching television together.

'As Aloysius became more and more fascinated by this strange group, they grew more and more fascinated by him. He wasn't exactly admitted into the bosom of the family. He had more the status of a family pet. When he entered the breakfast room in the mornings, the whole family would fall silent. They never referred to him as "you", but always as "Aloysius". Their formulaic morning greeting was, "Good morning, Aloysius," to which they insisted that he should reply, "Good morning, Ferns." To this they responded by asking in unison, "And how did Aloysius sleep?" Similarly, if the daughter, for instance, was asking him if he wanted more tea, she would say to him not "Would you like more tea?" but rather, "Would Aloysius like more tea?" It made him feel very curious. He felt it expressed respect, affection, and belittlement, all at the same time.

'The children competed over who would have the

pleasure of doing favours for Aloysius, taking it strictly in turns to offer him more toast, tea and cereal. The mother too insisted that he should allow her to serve him assiduously. Even the father would occasionally show him the courtesy of passing him a condiment or some item of cutlery, though because he was absorbed in his paper, and there being anyway such fierce competition to provide Aloysius with whatever he desired, he seldom succeeded in contributing much.

'All this attention Aloysius at first found embarrassing, but he soon learned to find it touching and amusing too. He still tended to keep out of the way of the Ferns for the rest of the day, though, finding the intensity of their concentration on his well-being rather exhausting, even debilitatingly so.

'At this stage none of the Ferns had ever touched him. There had been not so much as a handshake when he first moved in. Long after he had moved out, Aloysius recalled that he had never once seen them touch each other either, which in retrospect seemed strange in such an affectionate family.

'Sometimes, especially if he got up with alcohol still pumping round his veins from the night before, he would have a kind of waking dream at the breakfast table. Watching the Ferns smiling, circling around him, helping him to food, chattering about what they hoped to achieve during the day, moving swiftly about the table without so much as brushing against one another, he imagined them to be marionettes, automatons, or perhaps even ghosts, so precisely determined in their actions did they seem. Strangely, inexplicably, and as if by magic, their actions meshed together perfectly. They also meshed with what Aloysius said and did, which was even more eerie. On one occasion he even found himself trying to wrong-foot them by first thinking one thing and then quickly putting his thoughts into reverse and thinking the opposite, as if by doing so he could disrupt the pre-established harmony, which he felt could only be explained by some way they had of reading the contents of his mind. In this way he hoped to send the Ferns tumbling comically into one another, buttering the newspaper and pouring coffee on the TV. Needless to say, it didn't work.

'One day, when Aloysius had been living with the Ferns for several months, and Mr Fern was late home from work, Mrs Fern asked Aloysius very politely if he would mind helping the children with their maths. The son, Gordon, was studying for O-levels and the daughter, Trixie, for her As. Both were stuck with their homework, and Mr Fern would not be back until late. Mrs Fern herself knew no maths. Aloysius agreed. He helped them out, found he enjoyed it, and soon these little tutorials had become a regular fixture. Having recently studied the same subjects as Trixie, Aloysius found it easier to be of use to her than did Mr Fern.

'When these informal seminars had gone on for about a month, the time came around for Aloysius to pay his rent. As usual, he offered Mrs Fern a cheque, but she refused to accept it. She had spoken to Mr Fern about it, she told him, and to Gordon and Trixie, and they were all agreed that the tutorials he was giving them was worth at least what he was paying in rent, if not more. So if it was all right with him, she said, they would prefer not to accept any more money from him, just so long as he had time to spend a couple of evenings a week with the children. Aloysius was reluctant to agree to this arrangement, which threatened to put him in the Ferns' debt. But he enjoyed teaching the children, who were intelligent and fun to be with. And although his own parents were wealthy, they lived in fear of spoiling their children, so hardly gave Aloysius enough money to live on. In consequence he was very hard up.

'Any money he saved on rent might enable him to spend another summer adventuring abroad. After the tedium of nine months of medical lectures, the main purpose of which seemed to be to deter the weak-hearted from joining an oversubscribed profession, the idea of spending the summer working to pay off his debts was unbearable. And Mrs Fern went so far as to say that if he insisted on continuing to pay rent, the family would feel bad about taking up any more of his time. So, after thinking it through for a couple of days, he accepted Mrs Fern's offer.

'Mrs Fern was delighted, and immediately told Aloysius that the family had planned a special dinner to celebrate, which they would have the very next evening. They would be thrilled, she said, if he would share their meal with them. Aloysius told me that when Mrs Fern made this invitation his heart throbbed with an inexplicable terror. So perplexed was he by the strength of his emotional response that he couldn't make an answer. In the end he mumbled, "Yes," simply in order to extract himself from the room.

'This sense of dread worried him, for he could find no

satisfactory explanation for it. It had perhaps been a little presumptuous of the Ferns to plan the dinner before securing his agreement to the new arrangement, if that was indeed what had happened. And perhaps they had seemed a little overconfident about securing his consent. But considering how favourable the arrangement was to him, and how much kindness and thought they showed him day after day, these were minor indiscretions. It was perhaps also a little concerning that they considered his agreement to be a matter for celebration, for this suggested that they were to some degree welcoming him into their family, that they were beginning to consider him one of them, and that in future they might expect more in the way of sociability from him. But they had been so respectful of his privacy up to now, without him ever having to say a word to them about it, and they were after all such a close family, always so playfully scornful of outsiders, that he thought this extremely unlikely. And what did it really matter? If it came to it he could always go and live elsewhere. In short, there was nothing whatever to be scared of.

'So why this sudden feeling of dread? It was all the more inexplicable when you remember that Aloysius was more used than most to looking death in the face. He wondered if it perhaps wasn't fear he had experienced, but rather some kind of heart murmur. So he got a friend to give him an electro-cardiogram. This only showed that there was nothing at all wrong with his heart. In the end he decided that the only thing to do about this strange episode was to forget about it.

'He did so, and the next evening shared a delicious three-course dinner with the Ferns. Mrs Fern's cooking was excellent. Everyone drank the wine, which was well chosen. The children were delightful company, drinking just enough to set off their food without getting annoyingly drunk. Mr Fern and Aloysius remained at the table after the pudding and smoked fine Havana cigars, provided by Mr Fern.

'Aloysius told Mr Fern stories about his adventures on the Pacific island. Mr Fern listened politely, but Aloysius had the feeling that Mr Fern couldn't understand him properly, couldn't understand what he was doing in such a dangerous place. He kept offering his condolences on the holiday having been ruined, and saying other things that made Aloysius feel they must be talking very different idioms of the English language, though with identical accent and vocabulary. The meaning of words and phrases kept going astray. Mr Fern had to ask for clarification over and over, and Aloysius was constantly obliged to explain what he meant.

'Aloysius remembered thinking that at last the Fern family computer program had shown its limits, and that the truth was that Mr Fern was not all there. But then, ever charitable, he reflected that it could simply be that Mr Fern was nervous in his company, having grown unused to sharing anything more intimate than business small talk with anyone outside his immediate family.

'When they had finished their cigars Aloysius and Mr Fern joined the family in a game of Monopoly. At ten the Ferns retired, and Aloysius too went off to his own room.

'Being a little tired himself, and a little drunk, Aloysius decided to forego his usual late-night studying session and read a novel in bed instead. He had been reading for only about ten minutes when there was a quiet knock on the door. In the six months Aloysius had been living in the Ferns' home, this was the very first time any member of the family had visited his room. Still, that hardly accounted for the absolute terror he felt pounding in his arteries, stiffening the fibres of his muscles and making it difficult for him to remain seated in bed. He found himself looking around for a weapon. Then he took a hold of himself and said, "Come in."

'It was Mr Fern. He was not yet dressed for bed. Popping his head round the door, he looked towards Aloysius without really focusing and said, "Trixie would like to come in and share something with Aloysius. Is that all right?" His voice was weak and he sounded nervous, as though fearing the possibility of a humiliating rebuff. Aloysius, putting all his effort into seeming unconcerned, smiled and said it would be no trouble at all as he was awake anyway, reading. Mr Fern opened the door a little further and then promptly disappeared, leaving Trixie standing in the doorway dressed only in a short nightie.

'Aloysius felt a lump rise to his throat and his pulse quicken even further, as the dumb instinct of fear was augmented by a sudden explosion of sexual desire. Aloysius told me that when Trixie said, "Does Aloysius mind if I come in?" his penis went off like an airbag, becoming fully erect in a fraction of a second, feeling like it would burst with the pressure of blood. He nodded his assent.

'Trixie came in and closed the door behind her. "Would Aloysius like it if I got into bed with him?" she asked, with a tentative smile. Aloysius did his best to compose himself and to reflect on his predicament. The

JOHN BINIAS

bizarre fear was still there, accompanied by the wild sexual longing. But now these feelings were joined by something new. It was an incredible, horrified disgust. This disgust welled up inside him like the mystery of his birth, making him want to sneeze, piss, shit, laugh and cry all at the same time. He had never experienced such a cadaverous emotion in all his life. He responded instinctively, as he responded to all danger. He said yes.

'Aloysius described the sex by saying it was as though his entire body had become suffused with the sort of dense system of nerves that as a matter of biological fact is limited to certain mucous membranes, the tips of the fingers, the soles of the feet and so on. When they had finished, which took some three or four hours, Trixie went back to her own room and Aloysius fell into a deep, dreamless slumber.

'When he woke the next morning he tried to put what had happened out of his mind. He rose late, waiting for the whole family to leave the house before getting up himself. He made himself breakfast and was about to leave the house when he was gripped with the sudden desire to see Trixie's room. He had never been in any of the Ferns' bedrooms before, and as he knocked and entered Trixie's private space he felt a strong sense of transgression. He was shocked by the childishness of Trixie's belongings, the images of posturing pop stars, the fluffy animals, the trinkets, the family photographs, the adolescent magazines.

'He went off to university feeling not so much shocked by what he had done, which was after all perfectly legal, as baffled by the significance of it. He felt that he had entered some wholly new realm of terror. Lying face downwards on snake-infested vegetation with automatic rifle fire ripping through the undergrowth all around him suddenly seemed a rather tame and straightforward predicament. Befriending skittish cannibals whose language he did not speak seemed in retrospect a bit of a breeze.

'He said nothing to his friends of what had happened. He wasn't generally in the habit of discussing his sex life and, feeling some shame at what he had done, he felt no great desire to start making confessions now. Shame was an unfamiliar emotion for Aloysius. So unfamiliar, in fact, that for a while he wondered if he wasn't in love, for he thought of Trixie often, flushed a great deal, felt hot and sweaty, and suffered violent palpitations. He decided to stay away from the house until late at night, when he could get to his room without risk of bumping into any of the Ferns. But by the end of the day he was so exhausted that he decided he had no choice but to go home and rest. Once there he would lock himself in his room. If he went straight away he might just get there before they returned.

'To his horror, just as he was walking up the garden path towards the house, the Ferns' car pulled into the drive. He felt utterly perplexed and stood rooted to the spot like an idiot. But to his amazement the Ferns were perfectly natural with him, the children racing around him asking him their usual questions, the mother smiling her lovely warm smile and the father nodding to him engagingly, seemingly nothing short of delighted by what had happened. There was no suggestion of embarrassment, no hint that anything corrupt had taken place. Indeed, if anything the family gave off a feeling of relief, of purification, of having achieved some kind of renewal.

'Trixie herself made no acknowledgement of what had happened between them the night before, though she did have something of that extra confidence, that indefinable presence that clings to people for a short while after they have had a really thrilling sexual experience.

'Aloysius thought he should be delighted by the family's response, and especially by Trixie's silence on the subject, which he took to imply that she did not expect that their liaison would be repeated. But in fact he was devastated. He could hardly look at the Ferns, and though he tried to help them with their shopping, in the end Mr Fern and Trixie had to help him into the house, so weak and confused had he become.

'Mr Fern lay him on his bed and suggested that, since he was obviously feeling tired, he should sleep. Aloysius gratefully agreed. He slept undisturbed, again without dreaming, until around nine in the evening, when he woke sharply into a sweaty, heady silence. He could hear his lungs fill and expire, fill and expire, could even hear his heart's squelching beat. Outside and in, all was darkness. Then there was a quiet knock at the door. Aloysius guessed it must be a repeat of an earlier knock, and that it was the earlier knock that had roused him. He thought of springing up and locking his door, but feared that whoever was there would enter before he had time to reach the key, thus exposing him in his guilty intention. He felt that his best bet was to retain as much composure as possible, hiding the shame and pain that was brewing inside him. The door opened to reveal a slit of light. Someone spoke.

‘ "Is Aloysius awake?"

‘Aloysius recognized Mr Fern's voice. He was terrified, but this time fear seemed only to slow his metabolic rate, to quell his heart and dull his senses. He told me he felt like some ghoul, horribly scared by his predicament but unable properly to feel his fear, because in his heart he knew that it was he who was the ghoul, and that what he was really afraid of was himself. Eventually Aloysius admitted to Mr Fern that he was awake. Without opening the door further, Mr Fern spoke again. "Gordon has something to show Aloysius," he said softly. Aloysius didn't respond. He felt that the effort required to move his tongue in his mouth would be altogether too much for him. He needed all his strength to face what he knew was coming next, without simply dying of fear like a terrified rabbit. The door swung open.

‘There in the golden light of the hallway stood Gordon, dressed only in his pyjama bottoms. Aloysius had never found men or boys attractive in the past. He had indulged in some childish games at his boarding school, but had never thought of these experiences as sexual, since they lacked the emotional intimacy he associated with sex, and were more in the character of sensual experiments, as when boys cut their skin with a knife in order to see how much it hurts and remind themselves of what blood tastes like. But he had to admit to himself that he found Gordon attractive now. Once again his penis became engorged in an instant, and despite his exhaustion Aloysius felt his whole body shudder into vigorous life, just as it had the night before.

'Mr Fern must have been standing just behind the door, because Aloysius heard him whisper to Gordon to go straight in. Gordon did as he was told and the door was closed behind him. "Would Aloysius like it if Gordon got into bed with him?" the boy asked nervously. Aloysius didn't even think about his answer this time. As when descending a long, steep scree, a kind of controlled slide is the only technique to use if you want to reach solid ground without falling, Aloysius felt he had absolutely no choice but to concur in the boy's wishes. And he enjoyed doing so.

'The next day Aloysius did not have to make an effort to remain in bed until the family were out of the way, since he did not wake until it had gone midday. Again he had dreamed nothing, so that when he awoke he felt as if his soul had been borrowed during the night, or as if he had not slept but rather died and come back to life. He lay in bed for a long time, not feeling strong enough even to shower himself. He lay there quietly, trying to get his mind in order and to work out a way of extracting himself from this strange situation.

'First of all he would have to overcome the inexplicable state of febrility that had recently come over him, a condition that was becoming more pronounced by the day. He had no idea what, if anything, the symptoms might amount to medically, but he was convinced that the condition was related to the things the Ferns were making him do.

'But that was unfair. They were not making him do anything. He was doing these things of his own accord. No coercion had been used and his permission had been sought at every stage. He had no grounds whatever for complaint. So he could hardly ask for help from an outsider. If he told anyone about his situation he would only be laughed at, ridiculed and possibly imprisoned. How old were these children? He couldn't remember. They were certainly much younger than he was.

'Knowing that he still had some time to himself before the family returned home, he lay there on the bed, naked and unmoving, running through the situation in his head. But his predicament kept appearing to him in the form of a delirious chess problem, in which the pieces had no fixed value, the moves they were permitted to make altered from minute to minute, and the squares on the board changed their colour every time he touched a piece. He felt his brain burning, as if he were asking it to perform tasks that were no longer within its range of functions, as if his mental capacity had somehow been diminished during the night, his brain having slipped down a serpent on the snakes and ladders board of evolution, shedding the rococo folds of the cerebral cortex and the leaf-like laminae of the cerebellum, leaving him with nothing but the ancient, autoresponsive stem to manage on. The brain tissue he had shed was probably rotting in his skull at that very moment. That was why he had such a bad headache, and why he felt so enervated.

'When he reflected upon this conclusion, which despite its craziness gave him all the satisfaction of revealed truth, he began to fear for his sanity. This fear gave him new energy. Jumping out of bed, he showered and threw on his clothes. He knew now that he had to get away. He could go and sleep on a friend's sofa, even check into a hotel if need be. He would tell someone what had happened. He would confess every detail, to the police if necessary. He felt sure he had committed a very, very grave crime. Prison held no fear for him. He could still study there. They'd be sure to let him out for his exams. He'd just have to miss his summer holidays, that was all. It might even be a bit of an adventure in its way.

'He was about to leave his room and abandon the house for good, not even bothering to pack a toothbrush, when he heard a car in the driveway. He went to the window and parted the curtains a finger's breadth. It was the Ferns, all four of them. Of course, it was Saturday. They'd been to the ice rink together.

'Knowing it was too late to escape, Aloysius judged that the safest thing would be to get back into bed and pretend to be ill. If they thought he was ill, they'd leave him alone. Then, when they were absorbed in watching TV, something they did together most Saturday nights, he would slip out unobserved. He'd send a friend back to pick up his things later.

'So he undressed and got under the covers, dabbing his face with water to make himself look sweaty. He needn't have bothered. No one came up to see him. Why would they? They never bothered him in his room. Not during the day at least. They were very sensitive to the fact that he had a busy life of his own.

'He felt a fool. And he felt guilty too, for he had been unjust to the Ferns. They were fair-minded, straight-dealing people in their way, though their recent behaviour hardly fitted this mould. But could it be that in some way it was he himself who was making the family behave in this despicable fashion? They had been such extremely decent people when he first met them. What was undoubtedly true was that if he hadn't come to live there, none of this would ever have happened.

'Aloysius reached down beneath the sheets and felt his penis. It was slightly sore from the frenzied sexual activity he had engaged in on the previous two nights. Normally he would feel some pleasure at this memento of vigorous sex. Now he felt only shame and disgust. He felt like cutting the thing off and having done with it, freeing himself for good from the insidious demands it made on him. As he was reflecting on this idea, trying to make sense of all these new feelings, his cock started to swell in his hand. He let go of it with horror, as if finding himself with a human turd in his hand while swimming in some sewage-choked bay. But it made no difference. He was too late. His cock grew to its full size, and there was nothing that he could do to quell it. He desperately wanted it to go away, wanted his mind to be his own again. He started wanking vigorously, trying to get it over with. Once again he felt the now familiar feelings of panic and despair overwhelm him.

'He stilled his hand. What on earth was he doing, lying in a family home, naked, in the very bed in which he had recently ravaged the two virgin children of a man and woman who had shown him nothing but kindness, masturbating like a chimpanzee? He felt like crying with shame, with self-hatred, with revulsion. The only idea that attracted him now was suicide. But then, would suicide not be a kind of sexual act too? Is suicide not the ultimate act of onanism? Why could he not just stop existing? Why did he have to exist in the first place?

'In the end a bizarre plan came into his mind. He would go down and talk to the Ferns. He would apologize. He would tell them how he felt and he would beg their pardon for what he was and what he had done. He would not allow them to feel any guilt, because they were not to blame. He would instead take all their guilt on his shoulders, and then he would leave.

'He got dressed. His erection would not go away, so he put on two pairs of underpants and a pair of thick jeans in an attempt to hide it. As he walked down the two flights of dim, musty-smelling stairs to reach the Ferns' clean, compact living area, he felt great horror at what he was about to do. But for the first time since he had been with Trixie, he also felt some self-respect. This in turn helped him feel physically stronger. He had dreaded the steep, narrow top flight of stairs, thinking it only about a fifty-fifty chance that he would get down without his legs folding beneath him, sending him pitching downwards to break his neck against the banister. As it turned out he felt almost normal, only about as lethargic as the day after a tough mountain ascent, which saps all the body's reserves and leaves the muscles bruised.

'Arriving safely in the Ferns' private wing, he knocked boldly on the living-room door. His pulse was beating so loudly in his head that he could not tell whether anyone had answered or not. Taking a few deep breaths, he pushed open the door. Inside, the whole family was arrayed in front of the television. Mr Fern had the seat furthest from the set, but facing it most directly. Mrs Fern was on the sofa, knitting. Gordon was in the armchair nearest the television, and Trixie was perched on the arm of Gordon's chair, presumably delayed on her way to make a cup of tea by some interesting plot point.

'"Aloysius has come to watch TV with us," Trixie beamed out happily.

'"Would Aloysius like to sit here?" asked Gordon. "It's the best chair."

'Aloysius almost smiled. Such a warm greeting. Mr and Mrs Fern, too, had smiled at him with real affection. No, it wasn't just affection, it was love. Aloysius felt sure of that now. His head felt light. His erection was still thrumming inside his pants, but what did that matter? Nobody minded that here. But he mustn't forget what he had come to say to them. He had to clear the air once and for all.

'But how could he clear the air? It was already clear. Couldn't be clearer, in fact. Saying what he wanted to say would only pollute the atmosphere. What benefit could his miasmic fantasies be to anyone? Both these children were old enough to experiment with sex. The Ferns were an unconventional family, that was all. No, it was more than that. They were a family of genius. Genius is always unconventional, that's half the point of it.

'Catching himself reasoning in this way, Aloysius could feel himself about to give up. So he gave himself the biggest psychological smack across the face he could manage, reminding himself that he had come here with a mission and that he, Aloysius, never, ever went home before his task was completed.

'So he walked into the centre of the room and readied himself to address the Ferns as a group. But they had already gone back to watching the TV. Aloysius suddenly found himself too absurd for words. Mr Fern was craning his head so he could see the screen around Aloysius's bulging crotch. Gordon and Trixie were completely ignoring him. Only Mrs Fern was paying him any attention. Having half her mind on her knitting, she wasn't as involved as the others in the TV programme, but still Aloysius could see that he was annoying her a little by standing where he was, because she kept glancing up at him from her knitting. Then he realized that what she was really looking at was the bulge in his trousers.

'He was stricken with shame. His breathing became difficult, coming only in tight, asthmatic gasps. Then his eyes met Mrs Fern's. This eye contact almost made him stagger backwards, as if it had been a blow. Yet Mrs Fern was smiling pleasantly at him. Gathering her knitting in one hand and shifting forward in her seat, she reached out and put her arm around Aloysius's waist. Guiding him firmly but gently, as with a well-trained animal that only needs a hint as to what is expected of it in order to respond with obedience, she brought him towards her and positioned him on his hands and knees at her feet, so that he could watch the television without bothering anyone, and so that she could pet him while she was knitting.

'As she settled him, Aloysius felt Mrs Fern's hand brush casually against his erect penis. The gentle pressure on his turgid sex made him start. Mrs Fern responded by stroking him rhythmically and calmingly from nape to buttocks. Then, when he was relaxed, she reached under his tummy and loosened his trousers, easing them back over his hips and buttocks until they, and his two pairs of pants, made a slack ring around his thighs. Tickling his prick lightly under the glans with her long nails, she made it jump and buck like a little faun.

'Aloysius felt that this was all perfectly proper. It felt nice, and it was after all what he had come downstairs for. He could hear loose change rattling in someone's pocket. Looking round, he watched out of the corner of his eye as Mr Fern unhurriedly unbuckled his belt and dropped his trousers, keeping one eye on the television all the while. Aloysius turned back to face the TV himself. He too had started to become rather absorbed in the programme. It was about the wildlife in some unspoilt part of Africa. Aloysius felt something wet being smeared onto his anus and worked well in. He didn't bother to look to see who was doing it. It didn't matter, he was part of the family now.

'He shifted his weight a little to make himself comfortable. Trixie and Gordon looked round at him. They were gripped by the TV programme, but they were almost equally interested to watch their father expressing his affection towards their Aloysius. It would be their turn next. Unless of course their mother wanted to have a go. She hadn't had a chance to play with Aloysius properly yet, and that wasn't fair.

'By the time everyone had had their turn Aloysius was very tired again, so he curled up on the rug in front of the fire and slept. He must have been asleep for several hours because when he awoke, the Ferns had all gone to bed. The fire was off, but they had very kindly put a thick blanket over him, so he didn't feel cold at all. Guessing he had had no supper, they had left a plate of cold meat out for him on the floor. He ate the meat and then curled up again and went back to sleep.

'The next day the whole family drove to the countryside, taking their Aloysius with them in a big basket in the back of the car. He slept most of the way. He never seemed able to get enough sleep these days, or enough to eat. But the Ferns looked after him very well. They really did love him.

'The spring break had just begun. Aloysius's friends wondered where he had got to, but since they were all going home for the holidays, and Aloysius wasn't the kind of person who kept you informed of his movements, nobody bothered checking up on him. So for almost a month Aloysius lived with the Ferns in this way. He could have been living like that still, if it hadn't have been for the fact that a brazen young nursing student...' Nurse Sue paused here, and smiled coyly at her audience, so that they were in no confusion as to who she was talking about, '... who had fancied Aloysius like crazy for months and months, had at last managed to sneak his address from the faculty office.

'Despite Aloysius's inexplicable failure to notice her, this shameless young hussy plucked up the courage to go round to the Ferns' with a bottle of champagne, a packet of condoms, and the avowed intention of sacrificing what was left of her virtue to him at the first opportunity.

'But getting access to Aloysius was not easy. Mr Fern answered the door. The nurse, we'll call her Nicky, asked Mr Fern if she could see Aloysius. He went into the house, returning a moment later to say that Aloysius was asleep. Nicky scrawled a quick note for him, suggesting he should ring her, and then she left. He didn't call. So the next day she swallowed her pride, went back to the Ferns', and tried again, this time a little earlier in the evening. Mrs Fern came to the door, but the answer was the same. Once again Nicky left a note telling Aloysius that she had called. Mrs Fern seemed very nice, and at this stage Nicky didn't suspect that anything strange was going on.

'But on the third night the same thing happened again. Mr Fern answered the door, only this time when he came back to tell her that Aloysius was asleep he didn't seem to have been away for long enough to have had time to check whether Aloysius was sleeping or not. Afterwards, Aloysius said that he didn't think Mr Fern had been intentionally misleading Nicky, but that he knew very well that Aloysius was bound to be asleep. If he wasn't being fed or fucked, sleeping was the only other possibility.

'Nicky started to feel, how can I put it, a little fobbed off. She was extremely keen to get to know Aloysius better, she had come a considerable distance three nights in a row in order to do so, and she knew that if she didn't get what she wanted this evening she probably wouldn't try a fourth time. So she dug in her heels.

'Treating Mr Fern to her most austere look, she told him that although it looked like a social call, what with her wearing a short dress and carrying a bottle of champagne and everything, in fact she needed to see Aloysius on an important matter, and she would be grateful if he would go and wake him for her and ask him to come down. Alternatively, she suggested, he could show her to Aloysius's room and she would wake him herself, relieving Mr Fern of the responsibility for interrupting his slumber.

'Mr Fern seemed troubled by this dilemma. He hesitated for a few moments, then his mind appeared to clear. Without saying what he was doing, he smiled and walked back into the house, leaving the door open behind him. Nicky took her chance. Whether Aloysius wanted to see her or not, she was going to make sure she found out for herself. Stepping inside the lobby, she cried out at the top of her voice to Mr Fern that she had changed her mind, that it didn't matter after all, and that she was going now, thanks very much. Then she nipped through a half-open door into an unlit room, pulling the door to behind her. Her heart pounding, she heard Mr Fern return, walk out onto the steps, murmur to himself that she was a "funny girl", then come back into the house, closing the front door behind him. Then she heard him move away.

'Nicky had once made Aloysius tell her about the house where he was living, while trying to engage him in conversation in the refectory. She knew he had separate quarters from the Ferns, so when she judged that the coast was clear she went back out into the lobby and started trying to work out where they lay. The obvious thing to do was to take the route that Mr Fern had *not* taken when, she believed, he had *not* gone to check on Aloysius. So Nicky chose to explore up the narrow, musty staircase.

'This part of the house was unlit and not very warm. Nicky didn't have a torch, but she wasn't scared. It felt very uninhabited and she felt confident that she had gone the right way. The only danger seemed to be the possibility of giving herself away by standing on a creaking floorboard, or even falling through a rotten section. So she walked with very tiny footsteps, as though treading across a minefield. If the floor started to squeak, she quickly lifted up her foot and put it down elsewhere.

'Moving in this laborious fashion, she reached the top of the first flight of stairs and crept around the landing, trying each door in turn. Some were locked, some were open. The open ones she put her head around. She could smell whether the room was inhabited or not. She found nothing. Then she went up to the second floor. The third door she tried opened. The room smelt inhabited. It was very dark. She knocked quietly. There was no response, so she slipped inside. She listened for breathing but heard none.

'Eventually, when she had been in there for several minutes without her eyes becoming any more accustomed to the darkness, she switched on the light. It was Aloysius's room all right. She could see the medical textbooks and the sports equipment, and on the back of the door she recognized his jacket. There was no sign of Aloysius himself, though. Nicky sat down on the bed and wondered what to do. At first she had felt very excited and playful about her escapade, but now she began to feel a little shabby. What if Aloysius not only did not fancy her, but was really irritated to find her there? What if the Ferns found her first and threw her out? They might even call the police.

'Nicky began to feel wretched. Fearing imminent discovery she turned out the light and lay down on the bed.

Sneaking about a strange house in the dark listening out all the while for footsteps or a human breath had left her tired. She couldn't work out how best to extricate herself from this strange situation. She thought about walking straight out of the house. If she was caught she could simply tell the truth. But that was crazy. Heaven only knew what they might do to her. She could try sneaking out quietly. But then she wouldn't get the chance to see Aloysius, and all the fuss would have been for nothing.

'Suddenly, she sat up on the bed. She had it. She would open the bottle of champagne. If Aloysius hadn't returned by the time she'd finished it, then she'd sneak out of the house and go home. Fetching a glass from the bathroom and opening the bottle silently by letting the charge of gas escape around the tilted cork, she drank. Soon after pouring her second glass, she lay back on the bed and relaxed. Ten minutes later she was asleep.

'She awoke when the light came on. At first she didn't know where she was. She still had the bottle in her left hand, but it had tipped while she slept and champagne had poured onto the lap of her dress. In her other hand was her glass, still upright. She righted the bottle and sat up, blinking stupidly against the sudden brightness. Ahead of her she could see two figures. One was Aloysius, the other somewhat shorter. As the dazzle subsided, she could see that Aloysius was holding the hand of a young girl. The girl was standing a little ahead of Aloysius, as though she had been leading him up the stairs. Both looked perplexed, the girl in a surprised way, and Aloysius in a more fundamental way.

'Eventually Nicky was able to speak. "Hi, Aloysius,"

she said, managing to sound fairly casual. Turning to the girl she said, "Hi, I'm Nicky, Aloysius's friend. I'm studying nursing."

'The young girl smiled and said her name was Trixie. She looked up at Aloysius to see what he thought of the situation. He had a teeny-weeny smithereen of a smile on his face, as though recognizing something that was ever so vaguely familiar through a phenomenally dense fog. Seeing that he did at least recognize me, I decided to take charge of the situation.' Nurse Sue blushed slightly as her audience enjoyed her slip. 'That is, *Nicky* decided to take charge of the situation.

'So she went over and shook Trixie's hand, obliging her to let go of Aloysius's hand. Then she embraced Aloysius and gave him a big, champagne-soaked kiss on the lips. Aloysius smiled back dumbly. Nicky winked meaningfully at Trixie, told her it was nice to meet her, and showed her the door. Trixie left somewhat reluctantly. She seemed to be in a state of some confusion, as if she needed to say something but had no words to express what she was feeling.

'Left alone with him at last, Nicky made short work of Aloysius. Aloysius, who had grown accustomed to being made short work of, put up no resistance. When they had finished, Nicky stared into his eyes for signs of affection. Aloysius certainly seemed satisfied. If anything he was too satisfied, as he only wanted to go to sleep. Nicky gave him a prod and asked him to talk to her. Aloysius seemed surprised by this request. He lay in silence for several minutes, no longer inclined to sleep but finding nothing to say either. Nicky became frustrated. She repeated her demand. Aloysius reacted badly to this. Nicky's tone, which perhaps had been slightly harsh, seemed to hurt him inordinately, and he turned away. Nicky pushed him over on his back and stared hard into his baffled eyes. He really was hurt. She apologized, and a tear was born.

'Then, for the first time, Aloysius spoke. "Something strange has happened to me."

'They lay there together for hours as Aloysius slowly revealed his story. As he explained, bit by bit, exactly what had happened to him and what his life with the Ferns had been like, Nicky became more and more terrified. Meanwhile, Aloysius became more relaxed. No, not more relaxed. He was already relaxed, relaxed to an almost inhuman degree. He became more tense, more conscious. His sense of shame, horror and disgust at what he had become grew stronger minute by minute. Occasionally he would shiver as some recollection pressed itself upon him, before slowly and elaborately explaining exactly what it was that he had remembered.

'At first he was not able to distinguish essential from accidental aspects of his experience. Sometimes he would spend long periods of time struggling to choose between the warm attachment he had developed for the Ferns, and the nausea and repulsion that he experienced when he forced himself (or perhaps I should say "allowed himself", for it was far from clear which of his personalities was repressor, which repressed) to take the view of his activities that six months earlier would have been the only view he could imagine.

'Once she had a full picture of what had been going on, and Aloysius had expressed enough of his feelings to bring himself back to life a little, Nicky started trying to persuade him to leave the house with her. She locked the bedroom door and tried to dress him. But he was too much torn between these two conflicting states of mind to be able to act effectively. And convinced as he was that the Ferns would never use force against him, he did not share Nicky's sense of urgency. And it was true that the Ferns hadn't disturbed them so far. So Nicky resigned herself to waiting by Aloysius's side, listening to his stories of the orgiastic, bestial, affectionate domestic humiliation he had been through over the last few months.

'Eventually, in the early hours of the morning, Aloysius appeared to have completely caught up with himself, and to have gathered the psychic strength and emotional freedom he needed in order to attempt an escape.

'The two of them got dressed. Aloysius had grown unused to dressing himself, so Nicky and he did it together, giggling about his ineffectualness as though he were simply getting over a broken arm. Nicky borrowed one of Aloysius's coats to keep her warm. Apart from that, and the clothes Aloysius was wearing, they didn't take any of his possessions. Nicky was worried that if the family was still awake, and one of them were to see Aloysius leaving with a bag in his hand, a dreadful crisis might be precipitated. Far better to sneak out empty-handed. If they were discovered they could say that they were just going out for a walk in the moonlight. The family had never said that Aloysius couldn't have girls in his room, so they would have no legitimate reason for complaint.

'Finally they left the room. Nicky had to help Aloysius, leading him downstairs by the hand, just as Trixie had led him upstairs hours earlier. Nicky was as quiet as she could be, but Aloysius didn't seem able to prevent himself from making little noises as they went, drumming his fingers against the banister rails, taking childish little skipping steps here and there, and reaching up to set the lampshades swinging with his fingers as he passed.

'Whether these little noises alerted the Ferns, which perhaps is what they were unconsciously intended to do, or whether the whole family was anyway awake, listening out for signs of movement, doesn't matter now. However it happened, when Nicky and Aloysius reached the bottom of the second flight of stairs they found themselves being silently greeted by all four Ferns. Mother, father, son and daughter were standing in the hallway, each dressed for bed, each posted outside their own bedroom door, each illumined by a pool of warm light, the mother and father standing close together, the two children a little further apart.

'Nicky was terrified by these quivering waxworks, though she felt no violence or anger emanating from them. In fact she was surprised by just what a very ordinary family they seemed to be. Aloysius had described them as a family of genius, but in fact they seemed almost preternaturally normal, albeit a little vulnerable, and a little perplexed, and perhaps just a little depressed. But then family life often is rather depressing. Certainly Nicky could detect none of the extraordinary closeness, the team spirit, the forceful unity that Aloysius had described. Each Fern seemed to be looking out at Aloysius from their own separate world. The only thing that unified them was their common sadness, and perhaps fear, as they watched Aloysius being led out of their lives.

'As Nicky drew Aloysius towards the front door, she tried her best to keep her own body between him and the Ferns. They made a strange sight – warm, silent, anxious under flesh-coloured light. Nicky guessed they would be a painful temptation to Aloysius, and she guided him firmly. She had her hand on the handle of the front door when the dreamlike silence was finally broken.

'"Will you bring Aloysius back sometimes?" It was Trixie. Her tone was plaintive.

'Nicky didn't dare look back. Yes, she told the Ferns, she'd bring him back lots. They'd all go ice-skating together. This sounded unintentionally ironic, and for a moment Nicky feared that she might have roused the Ferns' anger. She fumbled with the lock, dropping Aloysius's hand in order to get the door open more quickly. Finally the door swung towards her. But where was Aloysius? She turned. He had not moved from the spot. He just stood there, gazing mutely at the Ferns, while they, a choir of angels entranced by the infant Christ, gazed back. Taking hold of Aloysius by both wrists, Nicky wrenched him out onto the front steps. They were free.

'As she drew the door closed behind her she couldn't resist taking a last peak into the house. The Ferns were standing in silence, staring eerily towards the door, their mood one of entreaty. They seemed to be hoping, but not believing, that she would keep her word. As she pulled the door to, she heard a last snatch of conversation.

' "Please, do come back..." Mrs Fern called out weakly.

' "Shut up, woman," Mr Fern barked.

' "Dad!" she heard Trixie wail in outrage. "Don't speak to Mum like that!"

'Nicky pulled the door shut, and gave Aloysius a big kiss to reward him for having behaved so well, a patronizing habit she was soon going to have to learn to give up. Taking him by the hand once more, she dragged him down the drive and out into the street.

'And unless you need to know how they found their way back to Nurse Nicky's flat, that's the end of my story.'

Nurse Sue sat down promptly, exhausted by her tale, and by the emotion stimulated by recalling the bizarre ordeal she had been through all those years ago. The people gathered around the table were silent, struggling to digest the significance of these strange events.

Eugenia broke the silence. 'What about his summer holidays? Did he go adventuring again?'

Nurse Sue, who was in the process of refreshing herself with swigs of rich red claret, shook her head. 'His taste for adventure was sated. He didn't feel that he could learn anything more from the experience of mortal danger.'

Strange to relate, but throughout Nurse Sue's extraordinary narration Mr Barclay had been laughing, sniggering, even snorting uncontrollably. At times he had seemed close to choking on his own guffaws. In the end he had resorted to sitting with his head bowed, as if paying

obeisance to Mirth itself, his hands concealing his reddened eyes and aching rictus like a pair of wrinkled old
crematorium curtains. Now the story was finished, he
recovered himself and sprang to his feet overexcitedly.

'What a tale. What a yarn. Thank you, and thank you
again. You have purged the poison in my blood. No
doubt it will return, the bacillus will breed, it usually takes
about ten minutes, but never mind that now. No doubt I
will die with a grimace of disgust for all creation besmirch-
ing my phizog, but while I have the enthusiasm to stand
and talk, while I have the urge to speak without simply
catapulting the germs of my misery around me in great
sneezes of woe, I must do so. I must speak now. Is it my
turn? Yes? No matter, I must speak in any case, or hold
my silence for ever. Good, I will speak. But I haven't
prepared a story...'

'Why don't you tell us more about Adman and Ivy
in the garden of Stink?' suggested Eugenia, with real
interest.

'Oh, God, not that old one,' objected Mr Barclay.
'Adman and Ivy stuck in the Garden of Stink, with very
little to distract them other than fresh fruit, sunshine, their
excretory functions and fucking, finally getting themselves
expelled when they offended God by asking him whether
pleasure was the best he could do for them. It's all too
familiar. Could have been anywhere, anytime. No, I'd like
to tell you something new. But since we all know that
that's impossible, I'll tell you something that sounds new
instead. Let me see ... I have it. It is the story of the
Ponce and the Pebble.'

The assembly expressed their delight at Mr Barclay's

felicitous choice of title, and urged him to begin. After supping off his wine and waiting for the glass to be refilled, Mr Barclay obliged. He spoke slowly and carefully, for he was speaking extempore.

(the Ponce and the Pebble)

'My story is a romance, a tale of frustrated passion besides which Tristan and Iseult will seem a lullaby to soothe sleepy lovers. It is a story of uncommon disappointment. But then perhaps it is not so uncommon after all, who can say?

'So, the Ponce and the Pebble. The ponce in question was a friend of mine, a purveyor of prostitutes by trade, and the scum of the earth to boot. A slothful, covetous, lecherous, lying, thieving, cheating, blackmailing whore-monger of a man, a thoroughly natural man, a man born with a talent for exploitation, a man ever vigilant for his own advantage and possessing little or no scruple as to how he achieved it. In short, he was in most respects normal. Except, when I think of it, for the birthmark on his face, which was shaped like a crescent moon, and so perhaps – who knows? – picked him out as destined to be a victim of unrequited love.

'The pebble was a beautiful little thing, burnished quartz with a delicate pinkish cast. He met her on one of his regular seaside excursions. I say "her" because he said "her", and for no other reason. For myself, I would not know how to go about sexing a pebble, or anything else for that matter. The ponce said "her" for the most obvious and traditional of reasons: that is, because the gender appeared clear to him. In his eyes this pebble was the very essence of femininity. Slightly pink, more noticeably so when wet, and with a perfect hourglass figure, she was alluringly passive, and her cool unresponsiveness power-fully suggestive of hidden depths. Her name was Delilah. To him, Delilah was all the more worthy of the rare and exquisite passion she provoked in him for having all of her clefts and most of her bulges permanently concealed beneath a translucent mantle of the most ethereal delicacy.

'These seaside jaunts of his were, it is probably worth me saying, of a professional nature. When one of his girls ran out on him, or got herself into trouble, or became infected, or, as the result of the persistent attentions of Old Father Time, grew insufficiently pert to please his clients (who were for the most part individuals of discrim-inating disposition, such as street traders, toilet attendants, politicians, and others of that ilk, all of them men who enjoyed soiling only the freshest and most doe-eyed of females) he would travel to a particular coastal resort, where he would pick up one or more bright-eyed trollops and have them shipped back to London, freight paid courtesy of their own gullibility, so to speak.

'He lured them on with promises of love, stardom, drugs, fun, or whatever snare they themselves professed an interest in. No doubt he would have baited his hook with promises of edifying trips round the British Museum, which vows he would have broken like all the rest, had he been dealing with that kind of girl. For his actions were motivated by the profit principle, and Kelvin, as I shall call him (for the word "ponce", though at first a source of delight to me, is now beginning to pall), had no intention of providing his girls with anything other than the bare necessaries of their trade, to wit, a pair of stilettos, a very short skirt, a boob tube, a handbag, and a bed, or possibly simply a stretch of pavement, depending on whether the girl in question had the quality Kelvin described as "class".

'Kelvin had spent a most satisfactory three weeks at this resort, having already arranged to transfer two vulnerable and unhappy young women to the capital, a would-be starlet named Gail and a girl called Heather, who only wanted someone to love her and look after her, an ambition which to Kelvin's mind was not nearly so reasonable as she seemed to imagine. Having done his work and made his arrangements, Kelvin was unwinding on the beach, enjoying the afternoon sun and inhaling a bit of fresh *luft*, before picking Gail up from her parents' house and taking her to the station, then collecting Heather from her bedsit ready for the drive back to London.

'He spent a little time lazily exploring a system of

caves that the sea, in its insane restlessness, had hewn from the base of a cliff. As ever, faced at close quarters with the brute emptiness of such esoteric spaces, which promise so much from afar but, when penetrated, reveal nothing more wonderful than the prospect of being drowned by the tide, Kelvin found his intrigue quickly give way to disappointment.

'So he left the caves, and was traipsing melancholically towards the water's edge, his eyes still accustoming themselves to the sheer weight of sunlight that was pressing hard upon them, when his mind was ruffled and his eyes touched by a pearlescent glister, an opalescent white fleck in the drab monotony of the shingle strand. He went closer to find himself face-to-face with Delilah. She was perched high up on the crest of one of the beach's tidal ledges, looking out to sea. Her beauty took his breath away.

'There were other pebbles on the beach, of course, many others. And it wasn't that Kelvin didn't see these others. No, he saw them all right. He even saw other white pebbles. And, if he'd looked hard enough, no doubt he could have found another pinkish moonstone with an hourglass figure and that certain way about her that set his heart pounding. But it wouldn't have mattered. Because for Kelvin, from this moment on, Delilah was all the pebbles in the world. She was, as it were, the idea or form of pebbleness. In short, she was Pebble itself, eternal Pebble, the pattern on which all other pebbles were based, and of which they were but imperfect copies, of infinitely lesser beauty and distressingly subject to the ravages of time.

'Whether, psychologically speaking, this sudden revelation, this uncharacteristic efflorescence of idealistic fervour, was a function of the lugubrious mood provoked by mooching around for too long in gloomy, prizeless grottoes, I cannot say. Perhaps it was in some way related to the deeper disenchantment that so often follows a successful seduction. In this case there had been two successful seductions, each repeated up to three times daily, giving a theoretical diurnal maximum of six ruttings, each followed by a facsimile imitation of post-coital bonding and tenderness. Taking into account the extra stress created by his secret intention of reducing these two objects of *faux* affection to a state of wretched humiliation for the sake of pecuniary gain, it is certainly possible to imagine that Kelvin's startlingly new perception of what was to all intents and purposes a perfectly ordinary bit of rock was very much the creature of circumstance.

'But who am I to judge questions of true love, I who have never even experienced the unreal thing? And maybe it was, after all, a more deeply rooted despair that produced in Kelvin this need for an object that, impenetrable and unchanging, would without a shadow of a doubt remain fascinating, mysterious and worthy of adoration until the end of time. Whatever the explanation, Kelvin was never the same again.

'When he first set eyes on her, Delilah was gazing out to sea. Kelvin, dapper in leather jerkin, faded blue jeans and brightly polished cowboy boots, found himself standing directly before her. But she didn't seem to see him. She had eyes only for the horizon, ears only for the whispered secrets of the sea. Kelvin decided to approach her by circling wide and then sitting down beside her with a smile, his usual technique when picking up women on open ground. He did so. For a long time he simply sat there beside her, drinking in the perfection of her form, relishing the translucent fragility of her skin. He was experienced with women, but was shocked to find that it took all his reserves of will-power to control the desire he felt for her astonishing beauty.

'To his mind it was clear that no one but a genius of seduction could ever hope to penetrate the defences of a female of such aloofness, and to enjoy her hidden treasures. With a quivering lip he decided there and then that he was the man for the job. If he wasn't that man already, he would do whatever it took to become him. With trembling delicacy he lifted up his sleeping beauty and carried her back to his car.

'At first he had high hopes. He imagined Delilah going all the way with him. Astonishingly for Kelvin, his horizons in this respect now extended beyond vaginal, oral, anal and group sex, to include settling down and starting a family too. For the first time in his life he felt ready for commitment, ready if need be to find a less well remunerated occupation, something more fitting for the spouse of a woman who possessed such natural aristocracy. But as the months passed he realized he had been naive. Soon his hopes had sunk so far that he would have been delighted beyond measure if only he could raise a smile from her.

'Knowing a thing or two about the psychology of love, having made extensive and duplicitous professional use of it during a successful pimping career that had lasted well over a decade, Kelvin was well aware that few people will love unless they first imagine themselves to be loved, or about to be loved, in return. For this reason he at first concentrated his efforts on lavishing affection upon Delilah, working his girls with exceptional toughness in order to afford for Delilah every gift, every sign and symbol of devotion a pebble like her could want. He provided her with companions both precious and semi-precious, adamantine servants of all shapes and colours, installing them in the velvet-lined jewellery box of finely wrought silver that he had acquired for her to live in.

'Delilah did not respond. Thinking that perhaps she was not happy with this accommodation, he bought her mother-of-pearl trinket boxes, caskets of spun gold, Fabergé eggs, brilliantly ornate mahogany jewel cases, more homes than a pebble could hope to occupy in a year. Still she remained indifferent towards him. He bought her eggcups to sit in, in a bewildering variety of designs, made from all imaginable materials, and had them lined with the finest silk. Surrounded by all this splendour, her natural beauty augmented by all this finery, Delilah didn't so much as blink, let alone yield up her secret soul to him. She did let him touch her. But she acquiesced in his caresses with such grim passivity that it was almost worse than if she had spurned him outright.

'And so Kelvin could not bring himself to persist with his advances. The last thing he wanted was to take this sublime goddess by force. He doubted anyway that he could manage such a thing. For although her beauty incited him, and her ingratitude spurred him on, her deathly calm was a tourniquet on the artery of his lust. She could not have shown less feeling for him if she had been made of wood.

'Eventually Kelvin acknowledged to himself what he should have known all along: Delilah was indifferent to worldly prowess and wealth, to the gewgaws of sensuality, to decoration and domestic abundance. She was, after all, an immortal, unmoved by things mundane, which come and go, passing in and out of being, possessing neither permanence nor perfection. Delilah could only ever feel passion towards the eternal things, such as high character, immortal deeds, and virtue, which as we all know is the greatest perfection a human being can aspire to, even if it is a little dull.

'And so the second stage of Kelvin's great courtship began. The first thing he did was to give up his business, flinging his girls out onto the street with no more ceremony than is merited by women who are willing to prostitute their bodies for gain. He left them to survive by their own devices, in which condition they were in every respect better off. Having thus rid himself of his shameful past, Kelvin threw himself wholeheartedly into the cultivation of the virtues. Guessing that Delilah was almost certainly a pre-Christian deity, he dispensed with Faith, Hope and Charity and concentrated instead upon Justice, Prudence, Courage and Temperance, together with a representative selection of the minor virtues and Aristotle's great favourite, Theoretical Reason.

'To encourage these dispositions to take root in the somewhat corrupt soil of his soul, in which until now a jungle of vices had flourished, and in order to learn more about Delilah's nature so as to be the better equipped to please her, he went to university to study geology. He studied Delilah's physical properties, including her crystalline structure, her chemical composition, her historical genesis, and the physical processes of freeze-thaw, exfoliation, attrition and possibly (though he hated to think so) trundling, that had all played their part in making her what she was today.

'Yet, in spite of these efforts, still her attitude towards him remained one of utmost reserve. Though sometimes in the early hours of the morning, after lucubrating hard all night, Kelvin did occasionally – oh lucky man – seem to see the iron-willed neutrality of her features flicker into the faintest, most ambiguous hint of a smile, giving an embryonic foretaste of the longed-for warmth and affection that he hoped she would one day share with him, when the sun rose she would prove as disinterested as before, and Kelvin would kick himself for allowing his rapture to overflow into fantasy, for her glacial indifference hurt all the more after he had imagined that he had seen it melting.

'As far as his practice of the virtues was concerned, things went pretty well. He was scrupulously fair and honest, always returned the balance when given too much change by a shopkeeper, did his quota of the cooking and cleaning in the houses he shared, governed his intake of food and drugs so as to produce physical health while at the same time encouraging the excellences of social intercourse, never shrank from a challenge, pursued his goals doggedly, and developed a habit of rational thought and action that, had he been living in a fifth-century Greek *polis*, might well have inspired awe and admiration.

'But as things were, whereas in the past people had in general found his desperately pragmatic attitude to questions of right and wrong repulsive, his contemporaries now found his scrupulosity absurd, pretentious and boring. And although some people were occasionally moved by his principled cultivation of the virtues to feel a little embarrassed by their own slovenly conduct, in the end they knew that, by basing their decisions on the twin principles of having fun and keeping out of trouble, they had the strength of numbers on their side.

'But Kelvin's zealous pursuit of virtue was in no way discouraged by this general indifference. Because Kelvin had a very practical end in view. He wanted Delilah to love him.'

Mr Barclay paused with a grimace on his face. He held up the palms of his hands, which had up till then been hanging limp at his sides, as though he had only just noticed they were there. As if trying to locate some sticky, irritating substance that was annoying him, he brushed the palms together, without, however, achieving any satisfaction. Then without a word he dropped his hands once more and continued with his story.

'Finding Delilah indifferent still, Kelvin started to indulge in feats of great physical endurance. He fasted for weeks on end, climbed great mountains, and endured hardships whenever he got the opportunity. But to Delilah's attitude towards him this made not one jot of difference.

'Thinking that he had perhaps been mistaken about her theological commitments, he resolved to train himself in the Christian virtues of Faith, Hope and Charity, taking a job in the City of London in order that he would be the better able to spurn Mammon by giving away his money for good works. He devoted his weekends to charity and spent his short evenings lay preaching. Yet still Delilah ignored him.

'Suspecting that he might have taken the wrong tack altogether, and that Delilah was in fact a thoroughly modern goddess who was turned on by individualism and personal expression, Kelvin gave up his job in the City and took a course in painting. Possessing some talent, a great deal of ambition and a bottomless well of hypocrisy, he soon proved a success in the marketplace. Still Delilah remained unmoved.

'By this time Kelvin was fifty years old and was considered by all who knew him to be a most remarkable man with an enviable list of achievements to his name. Yet all he himself could think of was Delilah, who spurned him at every turn, who in all the time he had known her had not once changed her expression towards him, and who was as unresponsive towards him physically as a woman imaginably could be. To Kelvin, Delilah remained what she had been on the first day he met her: she was perfect, and she was impenetrable. Now he found himself close to despair. Was the only thing he had ever wanted with all his heart destined to be withheld from him unto the grave?

'Then he understood. He had been hasty. Before she gave herself to him, Delilah was testing out his patience. So he took a job as a librarian in a provincial town and settled down, spending all his free time with her, talking to her, watching her, dreaming of her. In this way, ten more years passed. Still Delilah did not succumb to his advances. Still her disinterest burnt into his soul like a brand.

'On his sixtieth birthday Kelvin learned that he was dying of cancer and that he had only months, possibly weeks, to live.

'In his despair he went out and got drunk. Later in the evening he snorted some cocaine, visited a prostitute and beat up her pimp, just to show himself that he could still do it. He remembered the vicious pleasures that had sustained him when he was young. He had to admit that they had lost much of their savour, whether through age or desuetude, he did not know.

'When he returned home he feared that Delilah would punish him, that her attitude towards him would harden, just when he needed her sympathy more than ever. But though he confessed everything to her, she did not so much as flinch. It was at that moment that he realized it did not matter to her whether he lived a life of virtue or a life of dissolution and crime. He realized that Delilah was nothing more than a pretty piece of rock. He realized that his life had been squandered in chasing an impossible dream.

'For the first time in thirty years he saw the joke, and cried.

'Then, a few weeks later, he died a painful, humiliating and lonely death.'

Mr Barclay sneered unpleasantly. 'That is my story. It is pointless and ugly, but what did you expect? The man made a mistake. He believed the world had a hidden meaning. It does not. It is a pointless and ugly world we live in. A globule of sputum, hawked from the lips of a dying god into the eternal void. And we, the merest bacilli, remain.

'It is not forgiving of mistakes, this life of ours. Of mistakes or anything else.' Mr Barclay sat down. He appeared a little flustered. Embarrassed, perhaps, that he had been fool enough to start out his tale in such high spirits. No trace of that good mood remained. His face was bitter and contorted, his eyes screened beneath tight lids.

A sour silence ensued. Mr Barclay's listeners had been enthralled by his story, if a little bemused, and now they had been brought low by it. The silence was broken by Mrs Eugenia Quite.

'Why, when he saw the joke, did he cry and not laugh? It is usual to laugh at jokes, is it not, Mr Barclay?'

'Not that sort of joke, Mrs Quite. I have seldom seen people laugh at that sort of joke.' Mr Barclay defended himself against this challenge with bitter seriousness. Eugenia glared at him angrily.

'If there is a chip missing on my motherboard, Mrs Quite, then I apologize. If this hardware fault is occasion- ally relieved by some extraordinary input of data, some temporary software solution to my hard-wired deficiencies, that does not alter the fact that my system is not suitably configured for its operating environment. Maybe I am an evolutionary catastrophe. I know I am not much fun. But even so, I have given you my truth.

'If you care to take the ending of my story and give it another spin, turning my catastrophe into a careless joke, a cause for jumping joy, an incitement to cast off serious- ness, a liberation from the sinister doctrines of hidden meanings, deeper significances and romantic love, I wish you luck. I, as I say, have a chip missing, and cannot share your enthusiasm. But I hope I am at least liberal, and invite you to make of my narrative what you please.'

Mr Barclay bowed his head with uncharacteristic grace. Mrs Quite rose hesitantly to her feet, and began.

'When Kelvin realized his life had been ... squandered, in pursuit of an impossible dream, for the first time in thirty years he saw the joke and laughed. Still laughing, he took a train back to the seaside resort where he had first met this pebble of his. He took the pebble with him, wrapped in a hanky. When he got there the first thing he did was to place the little pebble back where it belonged on the beach. Then he blew his nose and walked away. When he had taken three steps he turned and looked back. He found he could no longer tell Delilah from the rest.

'His gaze freed at last from its extraordinarily narrow focus, Kelvin looked around him. He saw the sea frothing and spluttering fruitlessly, he saw the mute blue sky decorated with pointless delicacy by white cirrus clouds, he saw the inanimate mass of the silent cliffs, scarred and cracked beneath their own weight. He heard the outraged cries of the gulls and he sympathized. And then he smiled to himself. He smiled broadly.

'For he realized now that this impossible dream, this futile ambition, had led him to the most extraordinary existence. He realized that his longing for possession, an abject and necessary failure from the outset, had at the same time been a renunciation. And he saw that this renunciation had not been an unprofitable one. In the end, his useless passion was just one more way in which the world can be savoured. And so he wondered if perhaps he had not found more in his pebble than most people find in the whole world.

'He knew now that he had been wrong to take life so seriously, because life and death are both lighter than air. But would things have been better for him if love had not taken possession of him? Would his life have been better if he had continued to sneer at beauty, to consume it, to buy it and to sell it? Above all, Kelvin realized that he could now die with a light heart, die without fear of the void. Because the void was no longer banished in imagination to some mysterious other side, but was present in the world all around him. Indeed, he himself had become a part of it.

'In short, he had discovered that life has no interior, that the world is hollow and that we are hollow too. This was terrifying, but it was beautiful too. The terror and the beauty run into each other, just like the two faces of a strip of paper that is given half a twist and then joined up to form a loop.' Here Eugenia paused to tear a strip off one of the menu cards and demonstrate what she meant. 'The man saw this and he was glad.

'At last he had learned how to live. And though he was sorry to have so little time left to enjoy his wisdom, it didn't really matter because he also realized that in a way he had known all this from birth. He had remembered it just in time, because knowing how to live meant that he now knew how to die. And a few weeks later, after saying goodbye to the people who meant most to him, he did just that. He died an elegant and inspiring death, succeeding, as people occasionally do, in transcending the pain and the horror and the stench of terminal illness, flourishing in a way, even as he faded.

'This is the other end to Mr Barclay's story. Take your pick.' Eugenia smiled at each of the guests in turn, who were now mulling over her version. Then she took her seat once more.

She had not succeeded in driving out the mood of doubt, but she had at least shown her guests the other pole, reminding them of the painful, glaring white that stands as contrast and complement to Mr Barclay's consuming, shiftless black. Between these two extremes, the listeners were now free to choose.

Mr René Quite was cradling his head in his hands.

Mr Brian Smith nipped out to the lavatory. Mr Churchwarden was in the midst of a private colloquy with his dog. One or two of the other diners, finding Churchwarden's behaviour even more eccentric and incomprehensible than usual, exchanged ironic looks. One of these was Mrs Eugenia Quite, who now turned to Mr Churchwarden with a playful look on her face.

'It is your turn to give us a sermon now, Mr Churchwarden. Do your worst.'

'A sermon? Eugenia, whatever are you talking about?' Mr Churchwarden asked, eyebrows raised in surprise.

'I beg your pardon,' said Eugenia. 'I meant to say story. I don't know what I was thinking of.' Titters broke out around the table.

'A story . . .' mused Mr Churchwarden.

But Mr Brian Smith had now returned from the lavatory where, judging by his pallid, damp complexion and general air of surprised sobriety, he had been vomiting up much of the wine he had so assiduously glugged down during the course of the evening. He approached René and Eugenia Quite.

'I have to go,' he mumbled hoarsely, gagging a little on the acid in his throat and nose. 'I'm sorry. I've ... surpassed myself, you know. I'll have to go.' He was looking rather sheepish. René only nodded to him, but Eugenia was troubled. She took him to one side.

'Brian,' she said in a concerned undertone, 'you have to tell your story first. You really have to. The whole structure of the evening depends upon it. You promised me. Look, have a glass of water. You can go next, and if you're still feeling bad you can go home the moment you're done.'

Mr Smith hesitated. 'No, no, not water. Water's the last thing. Get me a brandy.' He hesitated again before returning to his seat, which he fell into clumsily. Wiping his brow with a napkin, he took out his little shorthand notepad and rapidly flicked through the pages, struggling to remind himself of the facts of the case. Eugenia watched him carefully.

'I think I have something,' warbled Churchwarden, 'something in the way of a parable, a little homily, you know, homemade, but nonetheless ...'

'That sounds great, Mr Churchwarden,' said Eugenia, 'but if you don't mind, Mr Smith will go first. He's in a hurry to leave.'

'Very good, very good,' mumbled Churchwarden. 'It will give me time to put my ideas in order.'

Eugenia thanked him. The guests were talking, dwelling

on the meaning of the stories that had gone before, and seeing to it that their glasses were refreshed with whatever drink suited their mood. Mr René Quite was eyeing Mr Smith anxiously, betraying signs of increasing agitation. Finally, after much sceptical huffing and puffing, Brian Smith stood up. The gathering fell silent.

(torments of remorse)

'I am not a talker, but a writer. And I deal not in delicately honed fictions, but in brute, ill-mannered facts, hard news for preference. So if my account is less than fluid...' Mr Smith tailed off, realizing that in such affable company no apology was required. 'Right then, I'll be brief.' His manner was businesslike, terse to the point of dismissiveness. He referred to his notes frequently, so that he rather resembled an insecure policeman giving evidence in court.

'An absent-minded university professor almost went to prison for murder recently after a bizarre series of mishaps and coincidences ended with him turning himself in, together with the partly frozen, decomposing body of a ten-year-old boy, at a police station in the seaside town of Scarby-at-Sea.

'It was only when police succeeded in identifying the body of the boy that the man was released. According to a police spokesman, the man, who had earlier confessed to murdering the boy, left the station with extreme reluctance.

'Doctors later revealed that the would-be murderer,' said Mr Smith glancing at René Quite, who stared back at him blankly, 'who cannot be named for legal reasons, had been suffering from psychogenic amnesia. This condition, which typically occurs in the train of traumatic life events, and has been known to result in sufferers "waking up" in foreign countries without any idea how they got there, afflicted the man after the break-up of his marriage. Around the same time he suffered a concussion sustained as the result of a fall, but it seems the concussion was the trigger for the amnesia rather than its cause.

'Tricking doctors into believing he was fully recovered, the man discharged himself from hospital and immediately headed for Scarby, where many years before he and his wife had spent a romantic weekend together. While staying in Scarby the man and his wife were briefly reconciled, but after catching him in compromising circumstances, she left him for a second time and his state of mind deteriorated once again.

'It seems the deceased boy had been drowned during a recent storm, when a freak wave washed him off the promenade. Despite risking their lives in the attempt, his father and passers-by had been unable to rescue the boy, who may have been knocked unconscious as he was swept over railings. The amnesiac discovered the boy's body on the promenade later the same day, while walking home from a party. For reasons which remain obscure, after unsuccessfully trying to resuscitate the boy, the absent-minded professor took the body back to his hotel, where he deposited it in a deep-freeze. The Grand Hotel in Scarby is now believed to be under investigation for offences under health and safety regulations.

'The man decided to give himself up following a second, successful, reconciliation with his wife. Despite its success this reconciliation seems to have caused his memory to play yet another cruel trick on him. Coming across a reference to the boy's body in his diary, and being unable to recollect the events therein described, the man became convinced he had killed the boy with a clawhammer. He handed himself over to police when what he described as "the torments of remorse" became too much for him to bear.

'The parents of the boy are quoted as saying they are relieved to have their son's body back.

'It is unclear whether the man will resume his academic career, which he himself is quoted as describing as mediocre.'

Brian Smith stood in silence for a few moments, flicking through his notebook to see if he had missed any details. Finding nothing, he nodded to his audience and resumed his seat. Unusually for him, he chose to drink nothing.

The effect this story had on the diners was mixed. The hotel proprietor seemed unusually anxious, possibly because he was reflecting on his ongoing problems with the health inspectors. Mr Barclay was regarding René Quite with something like amazement, admixed with a hint of admiration at the sight of a man who was capable of losing himself with such pertinacity. Nurse Sue was smiling affectionately in the direction of René and Eugenia Quite, favourably impressed by their unselfconscious eccentricity. Dr Nous was eyeing Mr Quite with something like annoyance, having learned for certain that he had been intentionally duped and feeling somewhat professionally humiliated. Eugenia Quite, having smiled her thanks to Brian, was now watching her husband carefully, trying to work out whether the time was right to encourage him to speak.

Mr Churchwarden didn't seem to have been listening to Brian Smith's story. At least, if he was listening, the story had made no impact on him. But he was a notorious deprecator of journalism, so either explanation was possible. Oblivious to the mood around him he now climbed to his feet, mumbling to himself under his breath as he did so.

'A story, hmm. Right then, yes.' Although Churchwarden was to some degree old-fashioned, in that he believed that there was a solution to the problem of despair, and was therefore a figure of fun among younger people, his dramatic presence, natural authority and eccentric appeal all asserted themselves, and soon every head was turned his way.

(reality isn't as real as it's
cracked up to be)

'My story is about a liar, a woman by the name of Pandora. She had all the gifts. Among these gifts was the gift of lying.'

'Is lying a gift, Mr Churchwarden?' said Mrs Quite loudly, pretending to be shocked.

'It is indeed, Eugenia,' explained Mr Churchwarden, apparently unaware that Eugenia was trying to make him look silly by pointing out his resemblance to a parish vicar. 'It is indeed. Possibly the greatest gift of all, and certainly the most problematic because, like all great gifts, it cuts both ways.'

Eugenia was pulling a little face, for the benefit of Effie Rance. It was a childish parody of the look of piety and love that Mr Churchwarden so often directed at his dog. Mr Rance snickered. Churchwarden saw this and his expression hardened.

'You ridicule my relationship with my dog, Eugenia. Do not think I haven't noticed this in you,' he said plainly.

Eugenia shrank with embarrassment.

'And, without wishing to dig myself any further into the mire of your contempt, to be absolutely honest I pity you for it. You imagine that you can live a full life with nothing but other human beings and your own creativity to sustain you. Many people imagine this. And they suffer the death-in-life of despair every day of their lives, until they are rescued from their torment by death itself.

'A friend of mine made your mistake, Eugenia. He made your mistake with a vigour and determination that you perhaps are not capable of. Yet it was a mistake nonetheless.'

Eugenia was looking down at her plate. She obviously felt rotten for being discovered in her callous show of disrespect towards Churchwarden, a man for whom she felt a great deal of liking. She looked as if she would have liked to apologize to Churchwarden for the personal offence she had caused him, but could not work out how to do so without betraying yet more contempt for his bizarre animalogical commitments, which she believed to be pernicious and dishonest. Her face glowed red, as shame and annoyance wrestled over her soul.

'Yes, listen to me, Eugenia. This friend of mine, a man who had for many years been deeply saddened by something without ever being able to discover what, thought himself liberated from his lugubrious torment by a brief affair with a woman.

'He had been in despair, not wanting to be himself, for he despised himself. And who, let us face it, does not despise themselves in this world of ours, that provides us with no roles from which self-worth might be derived, no fixed values to navigate by, no tried, tested and approved models of life, on which we might base our own?

'Early in his life, my friend Pascoe had looked into himself and found himself wanting. He should have got himself a dog. Instead he staggered on, gravely trying and rejecting one by one the ruses human beings use to kid themselves that they are not who they are. Traditionally, the next step in this dialectic of misery is to want to be yourself, that is to say, to pick out some collection of approved characteristics and cleave to them by sheer effort of will. The problem, of course, is that the self you want to be is not your real, dog's honest self, but a volatile concoction of circumstantial fantasy, very much like the transient self an actor creates and inhabits while performing a role on stage. This is exactly what happened to my friend Pascoe.

'He told me all about his affair as it was occurring. We were in the habit of taking a weekly walk along the cliffs together, I with my dog, he with his sorrow. Though he was a handsome enough man, with a reasonable income, personable, and with no obvious physical defects, he was amazed that this woman took such a deep interest in him. He felt she was too bright, too beautiful, too graceful to care about an ugly, miserable misanthrope like him. That's how he described himself. But it so happened that, just as he felt himself to be beneath this woman, so she felt the same way about him, imagining him to be far above herself in seriousness, intellect, forbearance and wit. And so that hackneyed old pseudo-miracle occurred, and each of the two felt convinced that a demigod had stepped down from the heavens to claim them as their own.

'For a few intoxicating months they became lovers, and lived together in a reality-defying condition of mutual admiration...'

Mr Churchwarden paused for a moment. In retrospect it was this moment to which those gathered around the table would trace the beginning of the astonishing course of events that was to follow. Not that anything untoward happened. And not that anyone could honestly claim to have seen in this moment a sufficient cause for what happened soon afterwards. All that the diners observed was that Churchwarden glanced round at his dog, which was at that moment sitting behind him and a little to his right. And instead of the usual look of beneficent calm, an awkward, lopsided look appeared on Churchwarden's face. Far from taking succour from the presence of his dog he appeared rather to be examining the doting hound as though seeing it for the first time. And when he turned back to face the gathering the lopsided look did not go away, but became if anything a little more exaggerated, as if the pressure of public recognition was developing and intensifying these incipient feelings.

Before opening his mouth again he swallowed hard and wiped his lips on the back of his hand. 'I had not meant to tell this story,' he said flatly, 'and don't know why I am telling it now. It is a painful personal memory, and the familiarity of years makes the pain no easier to bear.' Again he stood in silence, leaning both hands on the table, resting his weight evenly on all ten finger-tips, very much as though he were considering whether or not to attempt a handstand. For a moment his face relaxed, then the pain and confusion returned. The silence stumbled on.

'That is the way with stories,' said Dr Nous sagely. 'They are like lives: we never know where they might take us until they are ended.'

'Wise words, Dr Nous,' snapped Mr Churchwarden, showing more than a hint of annoyance at Dr Nous's ready phrase-making. His voice had taken on a slightly reedy timbre, and he looked and sounded more irritable than anyone could ever remember him. Like a man who had just received news of his dismissal from some time-honoured sinecure, his complacency was in tatters.

His physical appearance had changed too. He was normally somewhat baggy and ill-defined-looking, as though he were for ever seeping into his environment, and allowing his environment in like manner to permeate his own boundaries. But now he had lost all trace of this osmotic quality, his skin had become taut and sinewy and his face unusually pale. One of the diners remarked later that the overall effect was as if something that had been thoroughly steeped in some rich, life-preserving fluid had at last dried out, losing all its suppleness in the process.

'My story . . .' he continued weakly. 'My friend, Pascoe, later described the whole business as something like a conversion experience.

'We have all at one time or another allowed ourselves to imagine that we could make somebody happy by loving them, that we could transform someone's life by revealing them to themselves anew. This lucky person, we imagine, will be so grateful when we do this that they in turn will devote themselves to repaying the favour. Or, a little more realistically, we hope that they will become so dependent on the life-transforming spell that only we know how to cast that they will become bound to us, and ultimately forced to reciprocate . . .'

Churchwarden tailed off. Unbelievably, his dog had started whining and scratching at the leg of his chair. Credulity was strained even further when Churchwarden wantonly ignored this undisciplined behaviour. Finally, when Churchwarden saw that his audience was being distracted by the animal, he did something about it. What he did was wholly out of character. He turned to his dog and, holding an admonishing finger aloft, bellowed at it to be quiet. The dog collapsed to the floor, as though it had been struck by a heavy object. Then Churchwarden turned back to face the table and continued talking, in the same gristly, high-pitched monotone.

'Either way we hope that, by making someone happy, that person will become attached to us and come to love us in return. But this woman's admiration had such a powerful effect on Pascoe that the rest of the process just fell away. He inspired in her such passion, such deep and genuine admiration, that for a few hours, perhaps a few days, he himself became intoxicated by her view of him. It seems that in this short time he learned to see himself in a completely different light.

'Could she be right? At first he resisted the temptation to believe in love's phantasms, and told himself no. But when he reflected he realized he had no more grounds for that "no" than he had for saying yes. There were no grounds either way. The woman was not mad. She was not deluded. He had not concealed anything of himself from her. In fact, in order to avoid taking a nasty fall later on, just as one might be tempted to jump from a burning plane before it left the ground, he had been especially frank about himself. And still she thought he was wonderful. So why should it not be true? Why should a human being not be an object of wonder, of immoderate passion, of delight, of intoxication? And why should not he be just such a human being? He was no worse than many people. He was better than some.

'And so Pascoe was overcome with a vision of himself as loved. He described it as a kind of Christianity in which the Christ figure is cancelled out, as with something that appears on both sides of an equation. In other words, he explained, if you don't calumniate mankind in the first place, there's no need for an infinitely forgiving God to save your soul later.

'For the first time in his life he believed in the reality of human love. What had stopped him from believing before? He could not say. All he knew was that he had neither believed in other people's love for him, which he had presumed to be based on ignorance of his true nature, nor in his own love for others, which he presumed was motivated by a selfish desire to trick them into loving him in return.'

Yet again, Churchwarden paused. He looked at the upturned faces around him and licked his lips awkwardly.

'I can see that you are thinking that Pascoe and myself

are, or were, somewhat similar in this respect. Neither of us believed that human warmth, affection, respect, love was enough to sustain a life. I took refuge in my dog, Pascoe simply turned his face into the wind and trudged on.'

There was another long pause. Churchwarden was grimacing as though struggling to defend himself from the accusation he himself had articulated.

'So, the story. Pascoe realized that he had never in all his life dreamed that it was possible to be loved. Not for him, not for anybody. He just did not believe that humans had it in them. He thought them selfish and shallow and dangerous. Well, and are they not?'

This last remark was made with such bitterness that Eugenia actually flinched.

Churchwarden took a breath and continued. 'Yet now it seemed so simple to him. A case of the emperor's new clothes, only in reverse. That, at least, is how Pascoe saw it. He had been rapt by an image of himself, an image of ugliness, and the power of this woman's gaze had broken the charm. Her gaze was no more real or substantial than his own. Yet it gave him an alternative version, and he plumped for it.

'And so, after years of a grinding glumness that on many occasions had driven him close to suicide, not so much because of the intensity of his unhappiness as the sheer tedium of it, he was finally liberated. His sense of himself, the rock upon which his reality had been founded, vanished into thin air like a spirit at sunrise. He was no longer the person he had imagined himself to be.

'He explained all this to me one day as we walked

along the cliffs together. It was a fine, blustery summer's day. Fair-weather cumuli moved swiftly through the dizzying blue sky. Far below, an azure sea was chanting hymns of transcendence. That, at least, is how it seemed to Pascoe.

'"Reality isn't as real as it's cracked up to be," he kept repeating, over and over again. I explained to him that he was allowing himself to be taken in by an illusion, that the only place where love exists for real is in a man's relationship with his dog. When I said this, he smiled at me. I remember feeling patronized.'

At this point Churchwarden's dog found it impossible to put up with the lack of attention any longer. He just wasn't used to it. Jumping up onto his hind legs, he put his paws on the back of Churchwarden's chair and started barking eagerly, as though reminding his master of some treat he had been promised. For the first time anyone could recall, the dog was behaving like a spoiled mutt. Churchwarden, it seems, thought so too. Because, to everyone's horror, he turned around and without hesitation gave the dog a clout across the ear. The dog fell to the floor, whimpering pathetically. Then, hanging its head low and taking stiff, painful steps, it slunk to the far corner of the room. It seemed every bit as taken aback by Churchwarden's behaviour as were the humans present.

'I remember feeling rather patronized,' Churchwarden continued, oblivious to the scandal he was creating. '"Reality isn't as real as it's cracked up to be, Churchwarden," Pascoe kept repeating to me, like some crazed evangelist. Which is what you all consider me to be, of course. A crazed evangelist, I mean.

' "I don't mean that we won't die, or that pain doesn't hurt, or that sodium doesn't burn in water, or that dinosaurs aren't extinct," Pascoe said to me, his eyes burning like a pair of shooting stars. "I don't mean that at all. That's all real enough. It's me who isn't real. I've always thought I had to be myself, you know. I was clinging to myself as though I were some sort of safety device. I was unhappy with who I was, but still I had to be myself. It was as though I imagined my soul contained some sort of metaphysical parachute, and that all I had to do was to find the ripcord in order to be saved. Then that terrifying leap towards earth that we take every day, that plummeting fall into pain, death, loneliness and failure, would be transformed into a delicate, floating descent." '

Churchwarden stopped and looked around him. René Quite was resting his forehead on the table. Eugenia was looking fixedly at the tablecloth. Dr Nous was watching Churchwarden with professional blandness. Mr Rance was twitching and playing with the tablecloth like an unhappy infant witnessing a parental spat. Only Nurse Sue was looking on with something like friendliness, her face expressing a humorous compassion, which embraced even the unwholesome spectacle of an elderly man's spiritual disintegration.

Churchwarden took a deep breath and then continued. ' "Reality isn't as real as it's cracked up to be," Pascoe kept repeating to me over and over again. "I must have thought that if I clung to myself tightly enough this terrifying leap that begins every day on waking and ceases only with death would be arrested, and that I'd float down to the ground unharmed. What I didn't realize," he went on, now taking me by the lapels and speaking directly in my face, "what I didn't realize, and what I now know, is that there is no parachute, anywhere, for anyone. My problem wasn't that I couldn't find a way to arrest the fall, it was that I ever tried to stop the fall in the first place. Because life is a freefall, with a terrifying impact rushing up to meet us at the end."

'Suddenly, Pascoe released his grip on my coat and was running towards the lip of the cliff. He stopped at the very edge. "Life is a freefall," he shouted once again. For a dreadful moment I thought he was about to jump, but then I could see that he was only looking, contemplating his subject matter. After staring down in silence for a few moments, seemingly hypnotized by the maddening drop to the beach below, he turned once again to address me. He was calmer now. "Life is one continuous freefall. You're right to say that other people can't protect us, but dogs can't protect us either. The only thing to do is to abandon yourself to the excitement of it, Churchwarden. It's the only honest option. I can't believe I wasted all that time looking for a parachute when I should have been enjoying the spectacle. What a fool I was. Goodbye, Churchwarden . . ."'

Here Mr Churchwarden came to a complete halt. After a few moments, Eugenia asked him if he was all right. He nodded mutely. He looked very old and very crushed.

'So what happened, then?' Mr Barclay asked tentatively, giving a strong impression that he really didn't want to know.

Mr Churchwarden hesitated, then responded by picking up a large and suddenly very lethal-looking cake knife. This unexpected intimation of personal enfleshment left the

guests feeling utterly denuded as they scrutinized Churchwarden's eyes for signs of murderous intent. It was
Churchwarden who brought this speculation to an end.
Moving with surprising and not ungraceful speed, he
bounded over to the corner where his dog had curled up
and gone to sleep. The dog leapt to its feet, wagging its
tail with delight at the sight of his master. Churchwarden
rewarded this show of affection by taking the dog by its
forelimbs, tipping it onto its back, holding it down with
one strong hand and, accurate as a wayward veterinarian,
sliding the long blade between the dog's ribs and deep
into its heart. Uncomplaining to the last, the dog died
without a sound.

A fine spurt of blood squirted past Churchwarden's
head, painting a glorious carmine arc on the white wall
behind him. A vase of white lilies was also dashed with
red. And when Churchwarden stood up and turned to face
the table, it became evident that the stream of blood had
caught him too, because thick black drops of the stuff
were rolling down his cheeks and onto his white shirt.

The other diners regarded him with shudders of
horror. For a moment the dining room seemed like an
outer chamber of hell.

Churchwarden wandered back to his place at the table.
Though it was difficult to tell through the swiftly coagu-
lating blood, the colour appeared to be coming back to
his cheeks. Some of his usual porousness seemed to be
returning too. Wiping the blood from his eyes with a
napkin, he stood and addressed the gathering once more.
He spoke much more freely, as if something that was
caught in his larynx had now fallen away.

' "Goodbye, Churchwarden," Pascoe said to me. For a few moments I didn't know what he meant. We sometimes went our separate ways on the clifftop, following our whims, hiding from the wind or facing it, tramping on or wandering to our respective homes as the fancy took us. But Pascoe wasn't at a fork in the path, he was on the edge of a cliff, one of those spots where an eroded track leads directly into the void, beckoning us on to oblivion. I only understood his meaning a moment later when, with a comical little hop he stepped over the edge. He didn't cry out. He made no sound at all, in fact, not even when he hit the rocks. They told me later that his body was broken into pieces by the impact.'

Churchwarden was no longer able to stand. Eugenia helped him into his seat. He turned and looked towards his dead dog. One of the hotel staff had already started clearing up the mess. Rance appeared to be nervously contemplating the health and safety implications. Churchwarden called the employee over and handed him a twenty-pound note, asking the man very kindly if he would put his dog out where the rubbish goes.

Incomprehensibly, this request caused a ripple of laughter to spread and grow around the table. Giggles of relief, perhaps, but also the reflection of a certain mood that was developing, a mood of public solidarity worthy of the Colosseum. This laughter seemed to supply Mr Churchwarden with the strength to clamber to his feet once more. He now spoke lightly, haltingly, ironically, and with great respect.

'It seems my friend had a problem with gravity. That's to say, he no longer believed it to exist, or that it operated as constantly as it in fact does. The thing that had been pulling him down for all those years, you see, had disappeared. He must have made some kind of unconscious argument by analogy. Its effect was fatal.'

Now Churchwarden's energy really was spent. Sinking back once again into his chair, he leaned forward and rested his bloody forehead on the table.

There was silence. A curious atmosphere of expectation was developing, as though everyone was anticipating urgent news, but no one had any idea who the messenger would be, what the news might concern, or who might send it.

When the dead dog and the blood had been cleared away, the thing everyone had almost forgotten they were waiting for finally happened: Mr René Quite rose slowly to his feet. The guests were astonished that, after having held his peace for so long, he should find it within himself to speak. For a long time he stood in silence, looking straight ahead, as if watching the approach of some terrifying foe. When he finally spoke, the words he uttered were all the more powerful for this prefatory pause.

(Quite)

'Once he was happy...' said Quite.

'Never!' shouted Mr Barclay. 'Scoundrel, thou liest.'

'Yes,' retorted René Quite, 'and a thousand times yes. There is no greater gift. There is no other gift.'

'Then there is no lesser gift either. Call yourself a logician?'

'Life is the only lover of whom it is true to say, there is no other...'

'And she's a fat, farty old tart with gout and gonorrhoea and worse, and she doesn't understand us, and she doesn't listen to us, and she doesn't care for us, and she's not faithful to us. And so we don't care much for her. And I, for one, intend to leave her at the first opportunity.'

'And what do you know about her, other than through your own experience of her?'

'Nothing but what I hear.'

'Well, hear this ...'

Mr Barclay, disgruntled, immersed himself in silence. Mr Quite resumed.

'Once he was happy. The sun shone for him, the leaves on the trees murmured their greetings, and the birds sang iridescent songs. Each day, each moment of each day, had its lambent mood. The blue sky drew him aloft, grey sky confined him to earth, and the fluffy white clouds that scoot by in summer whispered to him of faraway places. Rain washed him clean, rivers thirsted for him, hills cowered and dales towered. The sea smiled, and if it frowned, frowned only in play. Pebble beaches counted a billion times a billion, birds swam heavily through thin air, fish flew weightlessly in the slow water. Gates were for climbing, songs for singing, food smacked its lips at him, and flesh cut. Yes, flesh cut, flesh seared, flesh hurt, but no matter, that was part of it all and he was happy nonetheless.

'One day, for whatever reason, he called out to his friends, to get their attention. But he couldn't call loudly enough, or else nobody was there, or else they just weren't answering. His voice resounded, hankering for a reply. Or perhaps it only whistled and whooshed ill-formed, illegitimate words. Who knows? Either way, there came no answer. In the end, tired of calling, he lay down. He lay down on some shady bank, or on some soft sofa, and fell asleep.

'He wasn't asleep for long. Perhaps it was no more

than a few moments. No longer than it takes to steal a human soul, in fact. And that's exactly what happened. He fell asleep and someone crept up and stole his soul. He sensed it the moment he awoke. Though the sun was still shining, he himself was shivering. His breath wouldn't warm his fingers, for it had gone icy cold. The blue sky, no longer infinite but flat, pressed down on him, or fell away from him, I'm not sure which. Either way it no longer drew him up. The grey sky dreared him, the rushing summer sky left him behind. Water sopped him, birds mocked him, fish rotted him, gates barred him. Hills reached up despairingly, valleys lay down and died. The leaves on the trees budded, grew, turned bloody and fell, over and over again without comment. Time counted. The pebbles on beaches unconsoled him infinitely. Meaning was meaningless, comfort comfortless, love loveless. Pleasure was lacking in enjoyment. He could see it, he knew when he was having it, but he could no longer feel it for himself. It made him want to give it away, give it to someone who could make better use of it. In short, he was disappointed.'

At this point Mr Quite's word-count suddenly fell to zero. Unable for the time being to weave more words into sentences, he looked down at the pink spider of his hand, which lay comatose on a tablecloth white as ashes. He seemed to be beholding the very winding sheet his warp and weft of spun terms had created. He stared, with questioning brow and parted lips, as though attending on the words. He stared and stared, and then he spoke once more.

'He didn't know who had taken it, but he did know

what to do. He put on his boots and set out on the trail, the little trail of fresh bright joy that had dripped from his soul as it was carried away. Because the soul had been immersed in delight for so long it was replete, and the thief could not staunch the flow, which poured from the point of detachment and drip, drip, dripped onto the carpet, the doormat, the pavement, the street, the open road. He followed the trail along wooded paths and moorland tracks, not stopping to sleep or eat or drink for fear that the flow of joy would eventually be stemmed, or that the soul would run dry and be lost for good, a discarded carcass.

'He walked and walked and walked. When the trail was strong he felt strong, and he didn't mind that his feet bled, his joints groaned and his spirit was dizzy with fatigue. But when the trail was weak he was weak, and in his weakness he despaired, tearlessly, of course. Then he would lie down on the filthy breast of Mother Earth and hug her, kiss her, sink his teeth into her flesh. But she gave him no succour. All he could do was sniff the air and move slowly on, his eyes caressing the ground for any hint of an ecstasy that might have passed that way. Then, out of nowhere, he would find a pool of the stuff, dark between two rocks. Then he would move swiftly on once more, confident that life was good.

'Eventually, after ten years, some say fifteen, he found himself at the top of a jagged, curling mountain road. He was exhausted, weak, and melancholy as the ghosts of vapour that wreathed the lonely peak like tired dancers. He could see where the trail turned off the road, passing over rocks freshly broken by winter's ravages, and on into a dry, scented wood. But he could move no further. He could barely even lift his thoughts. He slumped to the ground, panting. It was over. He was finished.

'After a while he looked around him, curious to see what backdrop had been chosen for the scene of his demise. Gradually, as though regaining consciousness after a fall, he saw how beautiful the morning would be, if only he could feel it, and he was filled with yearning, like a child's question.

'Once more he struggled to his feet and moved on, following his soul's spoor over the rocks and into the dry woods. Soon he found himself descending a steep slope, his feet crackling like flames on the dry twigs. His ragged clothes were grasped by low boughs as he pushed on, moving faster and faster between the trees. Then he stopped, alert. Ahead of him, between the lacework branches, in a shaft of orange light, he could see the thief, crouching over a mountain stream.

'It seems he had stopped there to don the stolen soul, to appropriate it as his own and reap his larcenous reward. And now, with two souls' joy to warm him, the thief was rapt, consumed by the beauty of the golden water as it tripped round rocks, wallowed in pools, sighed on high ledges, poured through the air, and sang out its greetings as it fell into its own arms. He had never seen anyone so happy as this thief was then.

'Picking up a rock, he moved forward. He made no effort at concealment, knowing the thief would never be able to look away from the water so long as the sun was shining. He paused behind the crouching figure, taking a moment to look at the brook, which fascinated the soulful thief but seemed to him nothing more than an ordinary everyday watercourse with little to recommend it beyond its power of quenching thirst. Then he bent over and dashed out the man's brains. The skull cracked like a seashell, oozing sacred fluids onto the lush grass. Both souls came free in an instant. He clasped them in his hands.

'The thief's soul he flung into the brook, for he didn't want a thief's soul for himself. It would live there harmlessly, giving a faint tang to the water and a slight mystery to the air around. The corpse he left for hungry animals to nibble on. Birds would eat the eyes, badgers the testicles, dogs the belly, something like that, it didn't really matter how. His own soul he swallowed immediately, cramming it down his maw like a hungry beast. As he did so, he saw the sunlight illuminated from within, and in the distance he heard the terrifying roar of a lion. All around him he sensed the trees whispering and the hollow air listening. He felt the warm breath of the earth against his cheek.

'Effulgence of white light. Pain embedded in warmth. Knowledge of joy at no distance. That is my story.'